He looked

Propped alongside his daughters in their bed, he was engaged in his nightly ritual of bedtime. The girls were sleepy as he read them a story.

Marissa took a moment to look at him, so handsome, so sexy.

She just stepped into the room when one of the girls said, "Daddy, we've been thinking."

"Thinking about what?" Grady asked.

"That we'd like to have a new mommy," she announced, so innocent it tugged at Marissa's heart. "And if you married Marissa, she'd be our new mommy."

The room was so quiet you could hear the proverbial pin drop. That's all Marissa could think of as the child's announcement echoed around the room.

Then blood rushed from her face and she gave a tiny gasp. Grady's neck snapped around and he looked at her. Stared at her. Through her. Into that place she allowed only him.

She waited for him to gently tell his daughter that it was impossible. That people only got married when they were in love.

What he said made her heart pound...

* * *

THE CEDAR RIVER COWBOYS:
Riding into town with romance on their minds!

Dear Reader,

Welcome to Cedar River, South Dakota!

Also, welcome to my eighth book for Harlequin Special Edition, *Three Reasons to Wed*.

I've always owned and loved horses, since they go hand-in-hand with cowboys. I'm delighted I can share my new series with you and tell the stories of the men and women who live in and around this small town, which sits in the shadow of the Black Hills.

You may have briefly met the hero, Grady Parker, in one of my previous books, *Claiming His Brother's Baby*. The widowed single dad definitely isn't looking for love, despite his mom's matchmaking efforts. But when Marissa Ellis returns to town, the handsome rancher suddenly begins to see her as more than an old friend. Of course, the path to love is rarely smooth sailing, and Grady and Marissa's relationship is no exception, especially with an interfering mother, three adorable little girls and a long-kept secret that will surely surprise everyone.

I hope you enjoy *Three Reasons to Wed*, and I'd like to invite you back to Cedar River very soon for my next book, featuring Grady's brother, Brant.

I adore hearing from readers and can be reached by email, Twitter and Facebook, or sign up for my newsletter via my website at helenlacey.com. Please visit anytime, as I love talking about my pets, my horses and, of course, cowboys, and I also share news about upcoming books in my latest series for Harlequin Special Edition, The Cedar River Cowboys!

Warmest wishes,

Helen Lacey

Three Reasons to Wed

Helen Lacey

Recycling programs
for this product may
not exist in your area.

ISBN-13: 978-0-373-65935-7

Three Reasons to Wed

Copyright © 2016 by Helen Lacey

Printed in U.S.A.

www.Harlequin.com

Helen Lacey grew up reading *Black Beauty* and *Little House on the Prairie*. These childhood classics inspired her to write her first book when she was seven, a story about a girl and her horse. She loves writing for Harlequin Special Edition, where she can create strong heroes with a soft heart and heroines with gumption who get their happily-ever-after. For more about Helen, visit her website, helenlacey.com.

Books by Helen Lacey

Harlequin Special Edition

The Prestons of Crystal Point

The CEO's Baby Surprise

Claiming His Brother's Baby
Once Upon a Bride
Date with Destiny
His-and-Hers Family
Marriage Under the Mistletoe
Made for Marriage

Visit the Author Profile page
at Harlequin.com for more titles.

For my lovely friend Kathi Hillier,
One of the best people I know.

Chapter One

Marissa Ellis pulled up outside her aunt's house in Cedar River and switched off the ignition. The old home looked shabby and tired. *Kind of like me.* But she quickly pushed the thought aside. For the moment she had more important things to think about than her own complicated situation. Aunt Violet was recovering from a fall and would be in the hospital, then rehab, for at least a month. Which meant Marissa needed to be in South Dakota to look after the small ranch.

It was the least she could do for the great-aunt who had taken her in following the death of her mother when Marissa was twelve. She'd spent six years living on the ranch. Until she'd finished high school. Until a scholarship meant college. After college, there was an internship at one of the most successful advertising agencies in New York, followed by five years of fourteen-hour days and multimillion-dollar deals. And then there was her husband. Who quickly became her ex-husband.

Marissa shook herself. There was no point in reliving all that now. She was back…for good.

The small town sat in the shadow of the Black Hills. It was actually two towns—Cedar Creek and Riverbend—that were separated by a narrow riverbed and a bridge and with a total combined population of a few thousand. A century ago, both had served as the backdrop for a booming silver mining industry. The mines were mostly closed now, with just a couple used as tourist attractions, and finally, after years of negotiating between the local governments, the town would soon be renamed Cedar River.

Marissa didn't really care what the town was called. She'd come back many times over the years—to see her aunt. To see her best friend, Liz. To see Liz's three young daughters. And then to attend Liz's funeral.

Never to see Grady.

He didn't like her anyhow. And since Liz's death nearly two and a half years earlier, Grady's disinterest in Marissa had amplified tenfold. Oh, he was polite and respectful and allowed her to see the girls, but he never encouraged her interactions and always seemed relieved each time she left to return to New York. But now she was back for good.

Her great-aunt's place was right next door to Grady's ranch, which meant she would have the opportunity to see her goddaughters more regularly than if she decided to reside in town.

If Grady continued to allow it, of course.

She'd have to see him, talk to him and make arrangements. But first, there was a house to settle into and sleep to be had. Marissa got out of the car and grabbed her bag from the backseat. It was nearly dusk and she walked carefully up the pathway, mindful of the overhanging branches from trees and shrubs well past their last prune.

The house was clean but smelled musty, and she quickly

placed her things into the spare room before she wandered through a few other rooms, opening windows to allow the fresh evening air to sweep through the place.

She made a cup of instant coffee and drank it black, since there was no milk in the refrigerator, and for dinner settled on the couple of cereal bars and the apple she had in her bag. Once she was done, she took a long shower and tumbled into bed around eight o'clock.

She tossed and turned before finally managing to get just a few hours' sleep, which left her restless and a little irritable when she was roused around six o'clock the following morning by a strange noise, like rustling bushes, coming from the backyard. Getting out of bed, Marissa padded down the hallway and opened the door to the small mudroom off the kitchen, peering outside. Dawn was peeking over the horizon and she blinked a couple of times to adjust to the sunlight.

And that's when she saw him.

Earl.

Grady's two-thousand-pound Charolais bull was eating the geraniums in an overgrown flower bed by the fence. She quickly saw where he'd broken several of the fence palings to squeeze into the yard and let out an irritated sigh.

Marissa shut the door, trudged to her bedroom, grabbed her bag and took out her cell phone. She had the number on speed dial and it took about three rings for him to pick up.

"Marissa?" Grady's deep voice wound up her spine like silk. "This is a surprise."

She took a sharp breath. "Your bull is in my yard."

"Your yard?" He was silent for a few seconds, but she could almost hear him doing that half-smile, half-frown thing he regularly did when they were around one another. "In New York?"

"At Aunt Violet's," she explained, her patience frayed.

He took another second to respond. "You're back in town?"

"I'm back," she replied quickly. "And your bull is eating the garden."

More silence. Marissa's skin prickled. Only Grady could do that to her. Only Grady could wind her up so much she wanted to scream. At eighteen she'd had a fleeting infatuation in him…but then he started dating her best friend and everything changed. It had to. Liz meant more to her than some silly high school crush. And when Liz and Grady got married, she stood beside her friend as her maid of honor and wished them every happiness for the future. And she'd meant it. Her own feelings were forgotten and she'd kept a handle on them for fourteen years. And she always would. No matter how much his deep voice stirred the blood in her veins.

Grady Parker was off-limits.

And he always would be.

"I'll be there in fifteen minutes."

The phone clicked and she took a long breath. Then she raced around like a madwoman looking for clothes to wear that covered more than her short cotton nightdress. Minutes later she was dressed in jeans and a bright red T-shirt and quickly ran a brush through her long blond hair before she hooked it up into a ponytail. She ignored the contact lenses case on the bathroom shelf and pushed her glasses onto the bridge of her nose. By the time she grabbed her cell and shoved it into her pocket, she heard a vehicle pull up outside.

Grady…

Marissa swallowed hard and headed for the front door. She spotted his truck and horse trailer in the driveway and felt the tension knot the back of her neck. She wiped her clammy hands over her hips and opened the screen door.

Seconds later he was out of the truck and walking up the path. Swaggering, really. With the kind of innate confidence of a man who knew exactly who he was. Grady Parker had always possessed that same self-assurance, even in high school. In jeans that rode low on his hips, a black shirt that stretched across broad shoulders, boots and a trademark Stetson, he made a striking image. He was about six foot two and as handsome as sin, with glittering blue eyes, dark hair and a whisker shadow on his jaw. He was cowboy through and through. With old-fashioned good manners and integrity.

But Marissa had no illusions about her relationship with Grady. It was tense, and always had been. When Liz was alive, Marissa had had her friend as a buffer. Now…there was nothing. Just raw, complicated tension that seemed to spring up with a will of its own every time they were within twenty feet of one another. He stalled about five feet from the bottom step and looked up at her, hands on his lean hips. They stared at one another for a moment, and as always her nerves sizzled.

"Hello, Marissa."

"Good morning."

He looked at the Volvo sedan parked in the driveway and raised a brow. "New York plates. You drove here?"

She nodded. "Yes."

His head tilted a little. "Have you seen Miss Violet?"

"I was at the hospital yesterday afternoon," she said, unmoving. "Thank you for taking care of things until I got here."

It was Grady who'd discovered Aunt Violet had fallen and broken her leg. Grady who'd got her to the hospital and stayed with her until she was out of surgery. And Grady who'd called Marissa to let her know her great-aunt needed her.

He shrugged. "No problem."

"I got here as soon as I could."

"I wasn't expecting you."

She straightened her back. "I told you I'd be here," she said stiffly. "I just needed a few days to sort some things out. I was coming back anyway."

"Really? For what?"

"To see my aunt," she said quietly. "And the girls."

At the mention of his daughters, his shoulders twitched. "Well, they always like to see you."

His words should have warmed her. But they didn't. Because there was a bucket load of resentment in them. Marissa pushed back her shoulders and stared at him. "Well, they'll be able to see as much of me as they like from now on."

He tilted his hat back. "They will? Why is that?"

"Because I'm staying."

"Staying?"

Marissa experienced a tiny surge of triumph. He looked as if it was the last thing he wanted to hear. "Yes. I'm home…for good this time."

I'm home for good.

It wasn't what Grady wanted to hear. Not ever. Marissa Ellis was the last person he wanted living in Cedar River. Or living next door!

For a long time she'd been living in New York. Out of sight. Out of mind. Just how he liked it. She'd turn up every now and then and he would deal with it because he had to. When Liz was alive, it had been easy—while Marissa visited, he stayed out of the way. Now it wasn't so simple. She was godmother to all three of his daughters and he'd promised Liz he wouldn't cut Marissa out of their lives. But he struggled with that promise whenever she returned.

Because once, long ago, he'd wanted to date her. Sure,

it had been in high school. Before he was old enough to know better. She was dazzling back then…with blond hair and brown eyes and a captivating smile. At eighteen he'd been fueled by hormones and lusted after the most beautiful girl in school. But Liz had set him straight when he'd asked her if Marissa would go with him to prom. It was a roundabout way to ask for a date, but he was a guy with all the usual insecurities. Liz had made it clear that Marissa wasn't interested. So he backed off and didn't ask her, despite how much he'd wanted to. Then he'd started dating Liz. And once school finished, Marissa left for college and New York. She would return a couple of times every year for a visit and he'd completely put aside the niggling awareness he had whenever she was near. He married Liz, had a family and forgot about the fact that long ago he'd wanted to ask her out. Life had turned out exactly as it should have.

Until his wife died.

"For good?" He wondered if he sounded like the simpleton he felt.

She nodded. "That's right."

"The divorce is final, then?"

"Yes. All done."

She'd been married for only a couple of years. Grady had met her ex-husband twice. Once at the small wedding that had taken place in New York, when he and Liz had left the girls with his mother and flown in and out of the city in just a couple of days. The next time, Marissa brought him to Cedar River for Christmas. He was a suit, as dull and stiff as they came, and had looked down his nose at the town and everyone in it. He hadn't come with her the next time she came back for a visit. A year later they were separated. Grady didn't know the details and hadn't asked. Miss Violet hadn't said anything about it, either, so he figured the less he knew, the better.

"I'm sorry to hear it."

She frowned at his words, as if he'd said something he shouldn't have. "Don't be," she said quietly. "I'm glad it's over. And I'm glad to be home."

"I didn't realize you still considered Cedar River home."

Her shoulders straightened some more. "I was born here…raised here…just like you. And you seem to have adjusted to calling it Cedar River."

He shrugged. "The merger is good for the town. And I know you were born here, Marissa…but I also know you left."

He saw her expression narrow, and the glasses on the bridge of her nose fell a little. Funny, he never knew she wore glasses. For some reason it pleased him. He couldn't figure why. Maybe because it made her less perfect. Vulnerable. Because he always felt as though he was under a kind of microscope whenever they were together. As though she was looking for flaws, some reason to dislike him. In a way he couldn't blame her. Their relationship had always been brittle, and for a long time he'd wondered if she knew he'd wanted to date her back in high school and disliked him for it. Liz swore she'd never said anything about it, and he certainly believed his wife. But there was something between them, a kind of mutual resentment that went deeper than simple dislike. Because it wasn't that he didn't like Marissa. He just didn't like to be *around* her. She put him on edge. And he didn't know why.

For years he hadn't thought about her as anything other than Liz's friend. He'd loved his wife. They had been devoted to one another and their family. But now Liz was gone and Marissa…well, she wound him up in a way he couldn't quite fathom. And he didn't like the feeling. Not one bit.

She crossed her arms and glared at him. "So, about this bull of yours?"

"It's because of Delilah."

She frowned and came down the steps. Grady caught the scent of her flowery perfume on the breeze and he tensed automatically. How long had it been since he'd noticed perfume? Years. Too long.

"Delilah?"

"Miss Violet's Guernsey cow," he explained and stepped closer. "She bought her a couple of months ago."

"I don't understand what that means."

"Well, Earl has a hankering for Delilah," he said and bit back a grin when he saw her frown deepen.

"A hankering?" she echoed.

"Yeah," he replied quietly. "You know, when-a-boy-likes-a-girl kind of thing."

She didn't look the least bit amused. "Right. So where is this cow now?"

"Miss Violet would sometimes keep Delilah in the backyard, but a neighbor has been looking after her since your aunt went to the hospital." Grady shrugged casually. "I guess Earl didn't know that. He drops over from time to time."

"Can't you keep him tied up or something?" she suggested. "I mean, how hard is it to keep him corralled or whatever it is you do with a bull?"

"And stand in the way of true love?" Grady put a hand to his chest. "That's not very neighborly."

"I'm not in the mood to be neighborly when the blasted animal is eating my aunt's flower bed."

Grady smiled to himself. Marissa was so uptight she looked as though she was about to pop. "I'll take him home," he said easily and turned back toward the truck. By the time he'd opened the side door and extracted a halter and lead, Marissa was directly beside him. "You planning on helping?"

"Not a chance," she replied and peered inside the truck. "You're the cowboy. Nice rig, by the way. New?"

He nodded. "Yeah," he said and immediately pushed down the irritation climbing up his spine.

It sounded like a criticism, as if she had an opinion about him buying a new truck and horse trailer. And she wouldn't be the first. He'd seen the same look on Liz's father and brothers. The same skepticism, the same query…as if they were looking for ways to question his integrity. Since he'd inherited Liz's money upon her death, there were plenty of people looking to see what he'd do. Sell out? Buy a bigger place? Add more cattle to the herd? He hadn't done any of that. Instead, he put the money in trust for the girls and got on with running the ranch as he always had. Business was steady and he made a good living. Good enough to run the ranch at a profit and take care of his family. The O'Sullivans thought way too much of their own opinions, and they'd never believed him good enough for Liz.

But he'd loved her. She was kind and caring and had been an incredible mother to the girls and an amazing wife to him. She was what he'd needed when his dad died and he took over the running of the ranch at just twenty. Liz supported and understood him. And he didn't regret one moment of the years they had together.

"Grady?"

Marissa's voice cut through his thoughts. "Right, the bull. I'll see he's out of your way."

"Sure," she said. "Can I see the girls soon? I have a few gifts for them. I missed being here for Breanna's birthday last month."

He knew Marissa was generous. And seven-year-old Breanna adored her, as did five-year-old Milly. Tina, who was only two and half, also seemed to light up whenever Marissa came to visit. And since he loved his daughters more than anything, Grady would do whatever he could to make them happy.

"Of course," he replied. "I had Cassie come around this morning after you called to watch them until I get back."

Her brows shot up. "Cassie?"

"My neighbor, remember? She's married to Tanner McCord."

Tanner was his closest neighbor and friend and was recently married with a baby and another on the way. Cassie McCord had been a godsend in the past few weeks.

She nodded as though her memory was kicking in. "Oh, right. What happened to Mrs. Cain?"

"Left last month," he said of his former housekeeper. "She moved back to Deadwood to be with her daughter."

"So the girls are eating your cooking?" she asked, widening her eyes provocatively. "Poor little things."

Grady grinned and curled the halter and lead in his hand. "They don't mind it. As I recall you're the only one who objects to my skill on the grill."

She gave a brittle laugh. "Skill? It's always raw. That's searing, not cooking."

He shut the door. "Let's not get into another argument about how to best serve steak, okay?"

Because he liked it rare. Marissa liked it well-done.

They never agreed on anything. Never had. Never would. The only link they had was Liz, and since his wife's death only his daughters had kept their association alive.

"Agreed," she said and followed him down the path and through the side gate. "And your bull busted some of the fence palings, by the way. So they'll need to be repaired. You can send someone over to do it if you like."

Grady got the message. Someone. Not him. "You're not much of a morning person, are you?"

"What?"

"Seems like you left your manners on the other side of the bed this morning."

She stopped in her tracks. "I did not. And I'm being perfectly—"

"Obnoxious," he said, cutting her off. "Give it a rest, Marissa. I know you had a long drive yesterday and you're upset about Miss Violet, but you called and I'm here. I'll take Earl home and get my foreman to come over and repair your fence, and if you want to drop by today or tomorrow to see the girls, that's okay. But can you ditch the attitude? I really don't have the time for it. I've got beef to get to market this week and I'm interviewing for a new housekeeper, and I don't want the kids to pick up on any tension between us."

She stared at him. *Glared* at him. And he waited for her to respond, to go on the offensive. To give it back to him in spades.

"Tension?" Her eyes widened. "Is that what it is?"

Grady shrugged. "I don't know. All I do know is that sometimes being around you is kind of exhausting."

When she didn't say anything, he left her and walked toward the bull.

Obnoxious? Attitude? *Exhausting?*

Perhaps she had been a little mean-spirited and irritable about the bull, but that didn't mean he had to tell her off about it.

She followed him, hands on hips, and watched as he effortlessly harnessed the bull and began to lead him across the lawn. He had a way with animals. Kids, too. She'd witnessed how much his daughters adored him on many occasions. Liz had adored him, too. And he'd adored Liz in return. Her friend had told her how much she'd loved being his wife. How caring and loyal he was. How faithful and strong.

Faithful? It wasn't a concept in marriage she was used to. Simon had betrayed her too many times. And within months of their wedding he'd cheated on her with a colleague Marissa had once considered a friend. In hindsight she knew she should never have married her boss, no matter how charming he had appeared. When she'd confronted him, he became verbally abusive, and later, that verbal abuse turned into violence. That's when she'd bailed, and she thanked her lucky stars she'd had the mental fortitude to escape. She'd told no one what had transpired. She had no one to tell. Liz was gone by then and she had no intention of burdening Aunt Violet with such knowledge. So she had stayed quiet and kept her problems to herself. She'd changed firms but Simon had already made it impossible for her to get the kind of position she was qualified for. He was top in his field, a true corporate shark, and pulled a lot of weight in a town where reputation was everything. And once Marissa's reputation was tainted, there was nowhere to go, no company that would take a risk with her, despite her stellar résumé and experience.

So, even before Aunt Violet's accident, she was planning on returning to Cedar River. She wasn't running away. She was starting over. Carving out a new life with new possibilities. To help Aunt Violet and fulfill the promise she'd made to Liz to always be there for her daughters.

And being at odds with Grady from the outset wasn't going to make that easy. So she sucked up her irritation and took a breath.

"I don't mean for us to always end up arguing, you know."

Grady stilled when she spoke, tightening his grip on the lead rope as he stared at her.

"You don't?" he queried and grinned a little. "It's the tension thing, then?"

Earl snorted loudly and she took a wary step backward. She wasn't much of a cowgirl. She didn't even know how to ride. Liz had looked awesome in the saddle, and she knew Grady's two oldest daughters had ponies of their own.

She dropped her arms. "It's just that we...we..."

"We've never gotten along," he finished for her. "Yeah, I know."

"But I think we should try, for the girls' sake," she added. "They mean the world to me."

"And to me," he said quietly, and she couldn't help but notice how the wind gently flipped through the hair at his collar. "And I do want them to know you, Marissa. There are things they can learn from you that they never will from me."

Mother kind of things. Marissa didn't miss the meaning of his words. Liz was gone and her daughters longed for a mother's love. She knew that. She'd felt it every time she called them on the phone and the last time she'd come home for a visit. Breanna in particular had craved her attention and had cried when she'd left. It was a memory that had haunted Marissa for months. And Milly...she'd been so close to Liz, and Marissa knew she missed her mother terribly. As for the baby, Tina had no memory of her mom. It was tragic all around. And since one of the last things Liz had asked of her just before she died was for Marissa to look after her girls, she knew she would always endeavor to do exactly that. Liz was her dearest friend and had been a lifesaver when Marissa had lost her own mother.

"I'll do whatever I can for them," she said earnestly.

Grady was watching her with such burning intensity she was tempted to look away. But she didn't. She met his gaze head-on. Steadfast. Resolute.

"Okay," he said and kind of half smiled. "I'm sure they'll appreciate any time you can spend with them."

"I could take them out tomorrow," she suggested. "Once I've settled in and stocked the house with some supplies. I thought I might take Breanna and Milly to see Aunt Violet."

He nodded. "Sure. You can collect them from my mom's around eleven. I always take them to her place Saturday morning."

Marissa knew that. Liz had started that tradition years earlier. And she liked Colleen Parker a lot, too. Grady's mother was one of those kind, forthright people who was always on hand for a cup of peppermint tea and a chat.

"Great," she said. "I'll see you tomorrow."

He nodded again and lingered, as if he wasn't quite finished speaking to her. "Yeah...right."

Tension returned and quickly filled the space between them. It was always like that. There was no remedy. No way of altering the fact that they rubbed each other the wrong way. It was instinct. Inescapable. It always would be.

"Goodbye, Grady."

He stared at her. Through her. His deep blue eyes were unwavering and intense.

"So long, Marissa," he said finally and urged the bull forward. He got to the gate and then turned. "And Marissa... it's good to have you back."

One brow rose. "You sure about that?"

"No," he said candidly. "Not one damned bit."

Then he walked through the gate and out of sight.

Chapter Two

"So...have you been seeing anyone lately?"

Grady rocked back in his chair and released a squirming Tina, who'd dropped her favorite stuffed frog on the floor and wanted it back. He picked up the toy and placed it into her arms.

He sat in his mother's kitchen, drinking coffee and having a reasonably deep conversation with his younger brother, Brant, about the other man's intention to purchase the Loose Moose Tavern. Or at least, what was left of the place after it had been partially gutted by a fire several months earlier. And he would have continued the conversation had his mother, standing by the western red cedar counter, not suddenly started grilling him about his private life.

"I see plenty of people," he said mildly.

Brant chuckled and Grady glared at his brother. He loved his mother, but when she got into one of her moods and started asking questions about what she saw as his lacking love life, a wall inevitably came up. Colleen Parker was a gem of a person and a wonderful parent, but sometimes she pushed too far and too hard.

"Stop being smart with me," she said and shook her head as she placed a sippy cup into Tina's hands. "Are you dating anyone at the moment?"

Grady cocked his head sideways. "Do you mean since you asked me this same question last Saturday?" He shrugged a little too casually and knew his mother wouldn't be fooled.

"Sarcasm isn't necessary. It was a reasonable question." Colleen came to the table and sat down.

Grady groaned. "Then no, I'm not."

His mother tutted. "How are you ever going to get married again if you refuse to even date?"

"I'm not refusing to do anything," he replied and sipped more coffee, keeping one eye on his youngest daughter as she wandered around the kitchen table. "I simply don't have time for dating. Nor do I want a wife at this point in time."

Colleen tutted again. "Your girls need a mother."

"They have a mother," he said, sharper than he'd intended, then softened his tone a fraction. "Just leave it alone, Mom. I'm fine, okay?"

"You're not and I can't," she replied. "I'm concerned about you and my grandchildren. And as your mother, that's my right. So stop fobbing me off with excuses like not having the time. You have to *make* time."

It was the same old song. The one he heard every week. For the past twelve months his mother had become unwavering in her belief that he needed to get married again. But he wasn't about to jump into anything. Sure, he knew the girls would relish having another woman in their lives... but marriage was a huge step. And he wasn't sure he had the heart to give part of himself to someone new...at least, not yet. He liked his life…most of the time. Sure, there were times when he got lonely, but who didn't? And there were nights when he would have liked someone to talk to, someone to curl up to and someone to make love with. But that didn't mean he was about to get into a relationship he simply wasn't convinced he was ready for.

He cracked a smile and looked at his mother. "Can't you point that Cupid's arrow of yours in his direction for once?" Grady suggested and hooked a thumb toward his brother.

Colleen grinned. "Once you're settled, he's next."

Brant groaned loudly. "Leave me out of this, will you?" he said in a despairing tone.

Grady looked at Brant, who was two years his junior, and smiled. But in his heart he worried about his younger brother, who had recently left the military after a third tour of the Middle East. Grady knew his brother had brought demons home with him. He wasn't sure what, but he felt it. Brant didn't say much. He didn't have to. They had been close all their lives. But something haunted his younger brother, something big. Only, Brant wasn't talking, and Grady worried that his brother never would.

"Not a chance," he said and laughed. "Now that you're back you get to take your medicine just like I have to."

They both laughed then and it felt good. He loved Saturday mornings at his mom's. The girls adored their grandmother and their uncle Brant, and having family so close by helped fill the void left when Liz had died. Despite Colleen's repeated matchmaking efforts, Grady knew his mom understood his need to keep his daughters in a loving and steady routine, without stress. She'd done the same when his own dad had died, even though he'd been twenty and Brant eighteen. Colleen had left the ranch twelve months later and moved into town, and Grady had taken over the family property. That was twelve years ago. Since then he'd married, had three children and buried his wife.

But his mother was always there. She'd been unfailing in her support after Liz had passed away and he knew he and the girls wouldn't have coped as well without Colleen in the background.

But it was getting harder to keep her at bay, despite her good intentions. His mother was relentless when she wanted something.

There was a knock on the door and he quickly got to his feet, happy for the reprieve.

Marissa...

It was eleven o'clock. One thing about Marissa, she was always punctual. He admired that about her more than he was prepared to admit. "I'll get it," he said and headed down the hall.

When he opened the door, his stomach did a sudden "Marissa is close" plunge. She looked incredible in blue jeans, a bright green sweater and knee-high boots. Her blond hair framed her face and her cheeks were flushed with color. Her caramel-brown eyes were unwavering as they met his gaze. One thing for sure, Marissa Ellis was beautiful. And Grady experienced a strong surge of something that felt a whole lot like desire sweep through his blood. He pushed it back quickly.

Not a chance...

He might not have made love with a woman since forever, but that didn't mean he was going to start thinking about Marissa in that way. That would be just plain stupid. And he wasn't a stupid man.

"Hi," she said, a little breathlessly. "I'm here."

"So I see," he replied and held the door back for her to enter. "The girls are waiting patiently in the family room. And on their best behavior," he added. "The promise of a day with you had them up and dressed at dawn. Now they're sitting quiet as mice—they've been watching cartoons until it was time to go."

She laughed and the lovely sound echoed down the hallway. He watched her walk, couldn't help but notice the gentle sway of her hips and the sexy-as-all-get-out boots. She had a style that was an intriguing mix of big city and small town. There was nothing obvious about Marissa; everything was understated and elegant. She was beautiful enough to grace a billboard but always looked just as much at home in jeans and sweaters as she did in a fancy suit or an evening gown.

Grady dismissed his wandering thoughts and ushered her into the kitchen. His mother and Brant both raised their brows when she entered, even though they knew she was taking the girls out for a few hours. His mom came forward immediately and drew her into an embrace.

"It's lovely to see you, Marissa. I was so pleased when Grady told us you'd come back for good. And Violet must be delighted."

"I hope so," Marissa said and hugged his mother in return. "She said you've been visiting her this week, so thank you."

"My pleasure," Colleen said and smiled.

"You remember Brant?" Grady asked.

She nodded. "Of course," she replied and flicked her gaze to his brother. "Nice to see you again."

"Likewise," Brant said, flashing her a grin as he sipped his coffee.

Grady watched as she made a beeline for Tina, who was now bobbing up and down with her hands outstretched. Marissa enfolded his child in her arms as though she was the most precious thing in the world, and something hot pierced his chest. It always moved him to see how attached she was to his daughters. Of course, Liz had been her closest friend, which would explain some part of it. And the girls were delightful. But there was an earnest, deep kind of love between Marissa and his daughters that rattled him in a way he couldn't quite figure. And she was one of the few people he trusted wholly and completely when it came to the care and well-being of his children.

As if on cue, Breanna and Milly raced into the room and shrieked delightfully when they saw her. She hugged them both while still holding the toddler, and he realized it had been an age since he'd seen the girls so happy. Marissa brought out the best in them, and from the loving expression on her face, it was clearly mutual.

Grady glanced toward his mother and saw how keenly she watched the interaction. He knew that look. *Great.* His mother liked Marissa…but the last thing he wanted was Colleen getting any ideas that included him and Marissa being any kind of *anything*.

He excused them to follow the kids and Marissa down the hall, then he grabbed the girls' bags from beside the front door, hauled Tina into his arms and headed back outside.

"I installed the car seat you gave me last time I was here," she said as they walked toward the car. "You know, the one for Milly," she explained as she unlocked the vehicle.

Grady was touched that she'd remembered. "Thank you."

Once they were all in her Volvo, she spoke.

"I'll have them back by four, if that's okay?"

"Sure. Have a nice time."

Then he waved them off and watched his daughters' delighted faces through the window as the car eased away. He took a breath and hugged Tina close as he headed back inside.

"And you, honey," he said as he kissed her head, "get to spend the day with Daddy."

She laughed and gently grabbed a handful of his hair. Tina was such a placid and lovely child. Not as serious and temperamental as Breanna or energetic as Milly, but more like her mom. She'd been six weeks old when Liz died, and it saddened Grady that she'd had only such a small amount of time with her mom.

Once he was back in the house, he made for the kitchen to collect Tina's princess backpack. His mother and brother were still sitting at the table, and both gave him an odd look when he entered the room.

"Marissa seems happy to be back," his mother said, her lips curling in a smile. "And it looks as though she's well and truly recovered from her divorce. She's such a beautiful woman, don't you think? And she's so attached to the girls. I know Liz thought the world of—"

"Mom," Grady warned gently. "Don't."

She sighed. "All I'm saying is that—"

"I know what you're saying," he said, cutting her off. "So just don't."

"I only—"

"No," he said, a little firmer. "Never. Understand? Never."

She nodded and stood, rattling the wedding band she still wore against the side of the cup in her hand. She was smiling. A typical Mom way of diffusing his impatience. There was no way he could get mad with his mother. She was all heart and the most generous person he had ever known. Even if she was set on interfering in his private life.

"Never say never." She looked at Brant. "That goes for both of you. Now, skedaddle out of here so I can get to my quilting class."

Grady said goodbye to his family and headed back to

the ranch, determined to get his mother's words and ideas out of his thoughts.

And failed, big-time.

Marissa had a wonderful afternoon with the girls. She took them to see Aunt Violet at the hospital and stayed for a while, then afterward they all got their nails painted at the beauty salon in town before going to the Muffin Box café for a shared plate of home-style sweet potato fries followed by pear-and-pecan-flavored mini cupcakes and vanilla bean milk shakes.

By the time she pulled up outside the ranch house, it was five minutes to four. Grady came out onto the porch, wearing jeans and a T-shirt that showed off his well-defined physique. He was broad in the shoulders and narrow in the hips and waist and well muscled. Not the kind of muscles from a gym as her ex-husband had boasted about…but from his years of working the ranch. From repairing fences and hauling hay bales and rounding up cattle on horseback. There was something so elementally masculine about him it was impossible to ignore. And the purely female part of her that registered an attractive man was on the radar was quickly on full alert, even if it *was* Grady. She'd have to be a rock not to notice he was attractive.

"Daddy!"

Milly was out of the car and up the steps in a flash, holding out her sparkly fingernails as if they were the greatest of treasures. She watched as Grady crouched down and examined Milly's nails and then ruffled her hair. Breanna was a little more subdued, but still happy to share the day's events with her father. She took out the girls' pink and purple backpacks, grabbed her own handbag and walked toward the steps. The girls were now inside and Grady stood alone on the porch. There was such scorching concentration in his stare she could barely handle meeting his gaze.

"I take it a good day was had by all?" he asked as he came down the steps and held out his hand to take the bags.

"Yes," she replied, suddenly breathless.

"Including you?"

She nodded. "Including me. They were very well behaved, even after I plied them with sugary food and drinks."

His expression narrowed for a moment and then he grinned. "I don't believe that for a second."

She shrugged. "I took them to the Muffin Box, so it was a healthy alternative. We had healthy cupcakes and soy milk shakes. I see that the O'Sullivans bought the place from the original owners."

"Yeah," he replied and swung the backpacks over his shoulder. "Too much competition for the café they had added to the pub, so they bought them out. Now they have the monopoly in town."

"Shrewd." She crossed her arms. "I guess they're happy about the towns merging?"

"They haven't any reason to complain. They own the biggest hotel in town and bought most of the commercial real estate on the Riverbend side of the bridge. A bigger, more economically viable town means more money in their pockets."

"I gather the relationship between you and them hasn't changed?"

She knew Liz's family hadn't really approved of Grady. He was a rancher, a cowboy, and they had wanted their only and beloved daughter to go to college. But Liz had been adamant. She had wanted to stay in the small town and become a rancher's wife. The O'Sullivans were old money from Riverbend, and as well as Liz they had three sons. One who ran the hotel and pub in town, another who was a doctor in Sioux Falls and the third who was a music producer in LA. It didn't matter that Grady's ranch was one of the largest and most successful in the county. They had wanted a certain life for their daughter, and since Liz's death their resentment had amplified. Marissa admired Grady's resilience, though, as he still ensured the girls spent time with Liz's parents and siblings.

"No," he said after a moment. "But I don't get so worked up about it these days."

"I'm not sure why they didn't approve of you. Liz said it was because they wanted her to go to college, but she was never all that interested in hitting the books. She liked to be outside, in her garden or riding her horse."

"Yes," he said, shifting on his feet. "She sure did look good in the saddle."

Marissa smiled. "I used to envy the way she could ride like that…sort of fearless." She crossed her arms. "Now I'm back for good, I should probably learn how to ride. Maybe I can trade some babysitting duties for lessons?"

His gaze widened. "You want me to teach you to ride?"

"Why not? You're pretty good on a horse, right?"

His mouth creased at the sides. "I do all right."

"And until you replace Mrs. Cain, you probably need all the help you can get in the babysitting department, right?"

"I guess so."

"You get a complimentary sitter and I get to learn a new skill. I'd like to be able to go riding with the girls. They were telling me today how much they love their ponies." She noticed he was watching her intently, and she wondered if she'd said something she shouldn't have. It was impossible to tell with Grady. "Unless you'd prefer I didn't. I mean, I know that was something Liz used to do with them and if you think I'm overstepping my—"

"I think they'd like it very much," he said, cutting her off.

She nodded. "Okay. Although, I'll probably end up landing on my behind. I've never been all that athletic. Liz used to beat my socks off in track in high school."

"Yeah, she was quite the athlete. But if it's any consolation, she used to envy your long blond hair."

"My hair?"

He reached out unexpectedly and touched her hair for a second, twirling a few strands around his fingers, then quickly snapped his hand back, as if he'd come into contact with a hot poker. The mood between them seemed to shift on some kind of invisible axis. And even though there was a breeze, Marissa turned warm all over. It stunned her that he had that effect on her—and it made her want to run. But she stayed where she was and sucked in a breath.

"She always wanted straight hair."

Marissa remembered Liz's mass of fiery red curls fondly. Once, when they were teens, they had tried to iron it straight. She still remembered Aunt Violet's despair at finding them in the bathroom, water running everywhere as they tried to douse Liz's smoldering locks underneath the faucet.

"Her hair was beautiful," Marissa said.

"I know that," he said and smiled fractionally. "She was beautiful inside and out."

There was pain and longing in his voice, and Marissa's heart constricted. "I still miss Liz every day."

"Me, too," he said.

Marissa's throat tightened. They'd talked about Liz many times during the past two and a half years, and yet she still felt the emotion rise up. It would always be like that. Liz was one of a kind. And her one true friend in the whole world.

"She was so…grounded. So sensible. Exactly the friend I needed as a teenager growing up. My mother had just died and since I never knew my dad… I guess that's why I was drawn to her. Her life was so different from mine, and yet we became firm friends. I guess she seemed to have this picture-perfect family."

"Nothing is perfect. Her parents put a lot of pressure on her. I think that's why she…" His words trailed and he grinned ruefully. "You know."

"Rebelled and married you? But she adored you."

"It was mutual. She made loving easy."

Marissa's heart tightened. She'd longed for that kind of love. She'd never seen it firsthand until Liz and Grady had gotten together and married. Her mother had raised her alone until Marissa was twelve, and Aunt Violet had never married. Her father, whom she only knew was some random cowboy who'd drifted through town, was never mentioned. Whenever she'd asked Violet, her aunt had told her to leave the past where it belonged. When she'd married Simon, Marissa believed she'd found the kind of love and family she was looking for—until he betrayed her with another woman.

Shaking off the memories, she focused on Grady. "I know she did. Liz had a great capacity for love…and a big heart."

"A weak heart, as it turned out," he said soberly.

Marissa nodded. The car accident that had landed Liz in the hospital was a result of a virus that had caused a massive heart attack. At just twenty-nine, she died three days later from a second attack. Six weeks after the birth of her third child, with her husband and family at her side.

"I'll always marvel at her strength that day," Marissa said quietly. "She knew… She knew she was so very ill, and she still made the time to talk to me and Aunt Violet. The last thing she told me was about you."

One brow rose. "It was?"

"Yes. She asked me to make sure you weren't sad all the time."

"Well, I'm not," he said and smiled. "The girls make that impossible."

"I know. And they adore you. You're a good dad."

He smiled. "Thank you. They adore you, too, by the way. I appreciate you taking the time for them today. Painting nails and cupcakes aren't really my specialty. Heaven help me when they hit puberty."

She chuckled. "I'm sure you'll do just fine. And it was my pleasure to spend time with them," she assured him. "I think of it as good practice for when I have kids of my own one day."

His gaze narrowed. "So, you want children? I thought you might have started a family while you were married."

A familiar pain lodged behind her ribs. "Simon didn't want children. Just as well, really, considering the divorce."

"That's a shame for him. It might have made him a better man."

"Nothing would have done that."

Grady's brows came up. "Really? You know, you never did say why you broke up."

Marissa shrugged. It was an old hurt she had no intention of sharing. "Irreconcilable differences."

"Because he was a pretentious jerk, you mean?"

Marissa laughed. "Something like that. I wasn't aware he'd made such a bad impression."

"Sure you were," Grady flipped back. "He called the town Hicksville and me John Wayne, remember?"

She laughed again. She did remember. Simon had complained the entire duration of their trip. He'd refused the invitation to stay at the ranch or Aunt Violet's and then had complained about the modest motel accommodation in town.

"I'm sure he would have been better tempered if the O'Sullivan Hotel hadn't been booked up that weekend. We had to stay at the Cedar Motel instead. It wasn't so bad, but he complained for three days straight."

"It wasn't booked up," Grady said and grinned. "Liz made that up just to antagonize him."

Marissa laughed again. "Bless her. It worked." She rattled her keys. "Well, I should get going. Thanks again for letting me spend the day with the girls. I hope they're not too hyped up to sleep tonight."

"I'm sure they'll be fine."

She was about to say goodbye when someone approached from around the side of the house. Marissa recognized Grady's foreman, Rex Travers, and nodded when he came toward them.

"Afternoon, miss," he said politely. "Boss says you've got some palings that need fixing." He removed his hat and tilted his shaggy blond head with a kind of old-fashioned cowboy respect. "I thought I'd come around Monday morning, if that's okay with you."

Marissa smiled. "Of course. I'll see you then."

"Around nine, if that suits."

"Sure," she said and smiled at the older man. He was in his midfifties and had a kind, weathered sort of look about him. He'd worked at the ranch for about six years and by all accounts was a good man with a solid work ethic. She knew Grady wouldn't tolerate anything else from the people who worked on the ranch. He said something to Grady about one of the cows and then ambled back toward the stables.

Marissa sighed. "Well, I'll be off."

He nodded. "Okay. Thanks again."

"No problem."

She was just about to open the driver's door when he spoke again.

"If you want to learn to ride a horse, I'd be happy to teach you."

She stilled. "Oh…sure. That would be great."

"Get some boots and a safety helmet from the saddlers in town. It's on the main street a few doors down from the old Loose Moose Tavern."

"I know where it is," she said. "And I saw the tavern today, or what's left of it."

He nodded. "Yeah, my crazy brother is thinking of buying the place and renovating it."

"That would certainly give the O'Sullivans something to complain about," she said and got into her car. Waving goodbye, she pulled away from the house.

As she drove off, she noticed he didn't move. He watched her, the colored backpacks still flung over one shoulder, his expression unflinching. And she didn't relax again until she pulled the car into Aunt Violet's narrow driveway. It was only a five-minute commute between the two homes, and from the corner paddock she knew it was possible to see the roofline of Grady's sprawling house.

She locked the car and walked around the cottage. There was a garden maintenance service in town and she made a mental note to call them on Monday to arrange for their help getting the yard back into shape. She'd talked to her aunt, and it looked as if it would still be at least three weeks before she'd be able to come home, if she came home at all. Aunt Violet had mentioned something this afternoon about moving closer to town, perhaps into one of the new retirement communities that had popped up near the hospital. If it meant selling the farm, then Marissa would certainly consider buying it. The cottage would look beautiful once again with some time and effort, and her aunt had suggested she think about doing something with the greenhouses Violet's older brother, Frank, had built years earlier.

Marissa had no memory of him but knew the place had been an organic farm once, so perhaps there was something she could do along those lines. Before she made any decisions she'd do some homework about the local economy and market.

Once she was inside, Marissa stripped off her clothes and took a long shower, then slipped into sweatpants and a long-sleeved shirt and made herself a cup of tea. By the time she'd finished puttering in the kitchen, it was past seven-thirty and she was about to settle in front of the television for an hour or so when her cell rang.

Grady.

She snatched up the phone and answered on the fourth ring.

"Hi," she whispered, a little more breathless than she liked. "Is everything all right?"

"Fine," he said, then stayed silent for a few seconds. She could hear Breanna and Milly chattering in the background and it made her smile. "Uh...the reason I'm calling is that the girls were wondering...well, they wanted to know if you'd like to...if you'd like to come over."

"Now?" Marissa asked quickly.

"No! No...tomorrow. Tomorrow night. For dinner."

Dinner with Grady and his daughters? He sounded as if he was swallowing poison along with the invitation. She took a steadying breath. "The girls want me to come over for dinner?"

"Yes...exactly."

"And is that what you want?"

Silence stretched down the phone line. "Uh...sure."

She'd bet the new boots she needed to buy that he didn't. "What time?"

"Six."

"I'll be there," she said, then disconnected the call.

Dinner with the girls—great. Dinner with Grady—she didn't want to think that it made her uneasy. Because that meant digging deep…and the less she did that, the better.

For his sake. And hers.

Chapter Three

There wasn't anything he could say to himself that would convince Grady that having Marissa over for dinner was in any shape or form a sensible idea. But the girls had begged him to invite her and he couldn't refuse them. They rarely asked for anything, particularly Breanna, who he knew missed her mother deeply. So if it meant being around Marissa for a few hours every now and then, he was happy to do it.

Sunday afternoon came around way too quickly, and by the time the girls were bathed and dressed and waiting patiently for her to arrive, it was past five o'clock. They could barely contain their excitement at seeing Marissa again.

She pulled up in the driveway at precisely three minutes to six, and as soon as she walked through the door his daughters bounced around, twirling and laughing, showing off their now-chipped nail polish. Once again he marveled at how easily and completely she captured their attention. Since their mom died, no one else could reach them the way

Marissa did. She had a certain kind of magic when it came to his daughters. Even Liz had known it. But he was pretty sure Marissa had no idea how much she meant to his family.

"Hi," she said when he greeted her in the hall.

"Hi yourself," he replied and stepped aside to give her room to pass. "We're eating out on the back veranda tonight," he explained. "The girls have already set the table," he said and winked slightly. "To celebrate your homecoming."

"Don't tell her that, Daddy," Breanna said and tugged at his shirt. "It's a surprise."

She laughed. "A surprise? I look forward to seeing it."

Grady grinned. "Don't say you weren't warned."

Tina grabbed his leg and begged to be held, and before he could pick her up Marissa held out her arms. "I've got her," she said and lifted her up. "I don't want to interrupt the cook," she said and pointed to the bright pink apron he had around his waist.

"Are you laughing at me?" he asked good-humoredly.

"If you want to walk around in that getup, you need to deal with the consequences."

"True enough," he said and plucked at the pink and silver sequins on the small apron tucked into his jeans. "But in case you were wondering, it actually belongs to Breanna and she insisted I borrow it while I cook on the grill."

Marissa raised a skeptical brow. "And it's not emasculating in anyway whatsoever."

"Gee...thanks."

She laughed again and the sound hit him directly in the solar plexus. She looked lovely in a knee-length soft denim dress and silver sandals. Her hair was down, flowing over her shoulders and down her back, and he remembered how he'd touched some strands the day before. He had no idea why he'd done it. He never overstepped the bounds of their often fraught relationship. She was Liz's friend. Not his.

And he didn't think about Marissa like that. He'd dismissed all those thoughts long ago, when he'd started dating Liz and fallen in love with her. But for some reason, one he couldn't fathom, right in that moment, with her beautiful hair flowing and her cheeks bright with color while she held his child as if she was a precious gift, Grady *was* thinking about it. And attraction, white-hot and completely unexpected, coursed through his blood with the speed of a freight train.

No! It can't be!

But he couldn't deny it. Couldn't do anything but let it wash over him and settle behind his ribs. He wasn't sure what to do with it. What to make of it. Or if he should or *could* do anything.

It will pass...

Of course it would. It was a fleeting fancy. Simply a matter of geography. Marissa was beautiful and familiar and suddenly near. Of course he would notice her. It didn't mean a solitary thing. And it didn't mean he'd be prepared to do something about it. If she knew what he was thinking, she'd probably get all outraged and call him a bunch of well-deserved names.

If and *when* he started dating again, it certainly wouldn't be with Marissa Ellis. They had too much history between them. They had Liz...and he wouldn't dishonor the memory of his beloved wife like that. Even if Liz gave the whole idea her blessing, which knowing Liz, she probably would have. The last thing she'd told him before she passed away was to be happy, to make another life, to not be alone. But he wasn't ready. Not just yet. And when he was, he'd find someone who didn't have a window into his past. Marissa was not for him. She might wield magic with his daughters, but he wasn't about to turn that into anything else. Anything more.

"Are you okay?"

Marissa's soft voice jerked him into the moment. "Sure…" he said and waved a vague hand. "Let's go out to the patio."

She followed him outside, Tina still locked in her arms. Grady watched her expression change to one of pure delight when she saw what Breanna and Milly had done to the long table. Dolls and colorful toys decorated some of the chairs. Bunting made from colored paper was stretched between the porch beams, and the table was decorated with glitter and colored glass ornaments.

"Oh…wow," Marissa said as she walked out onto the patio. "This is amazing." She looked at Breanna and Milly. "Did you do this for me?"

"Yes," Milly said excitedly and twirled a little. "We did it today. Daddy helped, too."

Marissa sighed and adjusted Tina on her hip. "Well, I have to say, this is just about the best decorated table I've ever seen. You've made me feel very special."

"You *are* special," Breanna said adamantly and grabbed Marissa's hand. "You're Mommy's best friend. So you're our best friend, too."

Grady fought back the lump in his throat. Of course. It made perfect sense. Through Marissa, his daughters stayed connected to their mother. They still felt as though they had her in their lives. Sadness lodged in his chest, sitting there like a heavy weight.

Marissa met his gaze and he knew immediately that she knew what he was thinking. Because she was thinking it, too. Her eyes shimmered a little, as if she was trying to hold her emotions at bay. He'd seen her cry once before—the day Liz had died. She'd gone into his wife's hospital room for a few minutes and emerged stoic and breathing deeply, until she'd made her way into the corridor. That's when she broke down. Grady was coming from speaking with the doctor and had watched her for a moment. He hadn't offered any comfort, because he didn't have any to offer. There were no words. His wife was dying and he had children he had to prepare to lose their mommy. But he'd felt Marissa's despair in that moment, right to the core of his being. At Liz's funeral she'd held it together, as he had. She'd given the eulogy and spoken about her love and admiration for her best friend. During that day, through his grief and sense of loss, he'd appreciated how she'd kept everything running smoothly—the wake, the funeral, even putting the girls to bed with a story.

Later, after everyone had left and his daughters were finally asleep, she'd made coffee and sat at the kitchen table. He'd joined her there, sitting opposite, sipping coffee he didn't want, wondering how he was supposed to go on, but knowing he had to for the sake of his children. In that moment, Marissa had shared his anguish as no one else could. She'd gripped his hand from across the table and held on and told him everything would be okay. And he'd believed her, trusted her, absorbed her words as if they were tonic. He owed her a lot for her strength that day.

Grady gathered his thoughts and ushered the girls away from her a little. "How about you give Marissa some space so she can relax."

"But, Daddy, I want—"

"No *buts*," he said to Breanna. "I'm going to cook dinner, so why don't you go and get that pitcher of lemonade from the refrigerator, okay?"

His daughter looked serious, but happy to do the chore, and took Milly with her.

Grady looked at Marissa. "You okay?"

She nodded and held the baby close before she placed Tina down so his youngest could play with the dolls strewn across the play mat. "Fine. Only…only I…"

"I know," he said when her voice trailed off. "They just about break your heart."

She nodded and sucked in a deep breath. "They miss her so much, Grady. I don't think I realized how much until this very minute. I'm in awe of how well you've managed these past couple of years."

He shrugged and moved toward the grill. "I've had help. My mom has been great and my cousin Brooke helps out with the girls when she can. And my best friend, Tanner, was always on hand right after Liz died."

She shook her head ruefully. "And I went back to New York."

"You did what you had to do," he said and placed the steaks on the grill. "Don't beat yourself up over it."

"I should have helped more. I promised Liz I'd—"

"You had your own life, Marissa. We all did. And Liz didn't expect you to hang around town. The girls are *my* responsibility, not yours or anyone else's."

Her expression sharpened. "Is that meant to put me in my place?"

Grady felt irritation weave down his spine. He always seemed to say things she took the wrong way. "It's meant to let you off the hook."

Maybe he did have the right intentions. And maybe he did have a point. But Marissa was still annoyed by the arrogance of his words. As if he knew what was best for her. The inference wasn't missed.

You should have stayed in New York...

"If you'd rather I didn't spend time with the kids, then just say so."

He put down the tray in his hand and turned. "You're here, aren't you?"

Marissa glanced toward Tina to ensure the child hadn't

picked up on the sudden strain between them and then she glared at Grady. "I'm here because Breanna and Milly want me here. I'm not under any illusions, Grady. I'm sure you don't want me one little bit."

His expression changed instantly and his eyes widened. How long had it been since she'd noticed how brilliantly blue his eyes were? Years, maybe. Over a decade. But now they devoured her with their intensity. Her breath caught in her throat and she swallowed hard. There was something hypnotic about his stare, as if she was being drawn deeper and deeper into it, into him. Marissa tried to look away but couldn't. He knew it, too. She was certain of it.

"Wanting you," he said, saying the words so slowly it was excruciating, "isn't the issue."

Marissa quickly realized how her words must have sounded to him. Intimate. Provocative. *You don't want me...*

"I meant that you obviously don't want me *here*."

"I don't?" he shot back. "Is that right?"

Breanna and Milly emerged through the wide doors at that moment and anything else he intended saying was clearly put on hold for the moment. Marissa plastered on a smile and chatted and played while Grady grilled steaks. Once he was done, they all sat down and Marissa watched as he put together a small plate of food for Tina and set her in a booster seat and got Breanna and Milly organized with their own plates. He was an exceptional dad. Caring and loving and exactly what she'd envisioned a father should be. She had nothing to test it against, no memory of a father or grandfather to make comparisons. But she could only think that if she ever had a child of her own one day, she'd like to share that child with a man who put his children above all others...a man who would protect his family with his last breath. A man like...Grady.

Whoa!

Marissa swallowed hard and pushed the notion from her mind. She had to. She had to forget that thought and never let it enter her head again. Because it was crazy thinking. Maybe she would get married again one day and hopefully have a child of her own…but it wouldn't be the man now seated opposite her. He was as off-limits as anyone would ever be. No matter how good a dad he was, or how sparkling his eyes were.

"Everything all right, Marissa?" he asked, watching her. "Steak okay?"

She nodded and dished some salad onto her plate. "Looks great. Just how I like it."

His mouth creased fractionally. "Well, I aim to please."

He didn't. They both knew that. There was nothing about their relationship that suggested either of them genuinely compromised when it came to one another. He would have been happier cooking her the rarest steak of the century and then telling her to deal with it. But he didn't. Instead, he pretended interest in his food and chatted to his daughters. But Marissa wasn't fooled. There was an undercurrent of tension whispering on the air between them, and she knew he felt it as much as she did.

Once they'd finished eating, the girls lingered over their plates and played with a couple of the dolls that decorated the table. At seven, Grady excused himself to put Tina to bed, and by the time he returned Marissa had cleared the table and was stacking the dishwasher. Breanna and Milly helped and she marveled at how easy the whole scene was—as though she'd done it a thousand times before. In that moment she felt a profound sense of loss for her best friend and said a silent prayer to Liz for allowing her to spend time with her precious daughters. Of course, it was Grady's doing really, but the gratitude she experienced deep through to her bones made her uncomfortable. She still couldn't bring herself to acknowledge it to him.

When Grady came back into the kitchen, he told the girls to kiss Marissa good-night and then to hightail it to their bedroom with the promise of a story before they went to sleep.

"You've cleaned up?" he remarked once the girls skipped from the room.

Marissa shrugged. "Seemed like the least I could do, since you cooked."

She noticed the pink apron was gone but there was glitter on his shirt and jeans. As she looked him over, a strange sensation hit the pit of her stomach. She couldn't define the feeling. It wasn't simply a reaction to his good looks. After all, she'd known good-looking men before. He ex-husband had been as handsome as anything. But Grady was different. He was confident but not cocky. He was also immensely likable even though it always seemed as though they were at odds with one another. Back in high school they'd been friendly, but not friends. She'd always been a little on edge around him, always conscious of the awareness that thrummed through her whenever he was near. Once he'd started dating Liz, though, she pushed those feelings aside, never willing to admit that her heart had broken just a little. But she'd loved Liz and would never had said or done anything that might have hurt her best friend. And she'd gotten over her harmless crush.

Or so she thought…

Because in that moment, he looked so good in low-riding jeans and a navy polo shirt, Marissa was forced to admit that she did find him attractive. Very much so.

"Coffee?" she asked, aware that it sounded more like a squeak than a question.

"Sure," he said and came around the kitchen counter.

"But I'll make it. Do you want to read the girls a story before they go to sleep?"

Her eyes widened. "Really? I'd love to."

He nodded. "Go ahead."

She disappeared quickly—anything to get away from him in that moment. The kitchen had suddenly grown smaller, the air thicker. Panic set alight across her skin and she lingered in the bedroom with the girls, determined to get her foolish thoughts from her mind. She read them a story about castles and princesses and tucked them in tightly when she was done.

When she returned to the kitchen, he was sitting at the big round table, coffee mug between his hands, and he looked up when she entered. "Are they asleep?"

"Dozing," she replied. "I said you'd be in a little later to say good-night." Marissa took a breath and straightened her back. "Well, I guess I should probably get going. It's a school night and—"

"Not for me," he said and raised a brow and motioned to the other mug on the table. "Or you."

She nodded slowly and sat down. The room was quiet, except for a clock ticking methodically on the wall and the infrequent sound of insects outside. It was a simple moment that suddenly seemed as complicated as anything ever had in her life. And she didn't know why. She wasn't sure what the intense tension between them was all about. In the past she'd been able to ignore it. But not now.

"Grady, I—"

"Why'd you get divorced?"

It wasn't a question she'd been expecting. Grady had never asked her personal questions, not in all the years they'd known one another. Liz had been her confidante. Her friend. In some ways very much her soul mate. It was a friendship she deeply missed.

"He was…unfaithful."

There. It was out. For the first time. Without Liz to confide in, Marissa had felt very much alone since she'd discovered Simon had been with another woman. With several, in fact, pretty much from the onset of their marriage. Saying the words felt good.

Grady raised his mug and stared at her over the rim. "Unworthy bastard."

Emotion clogged her throat. "Yes…that's a good way of putting it."

"You're well rid of him, then?"

She nodded. "I guess I am."

His gaze narrowed. "Do you still love him?"

"No."

He looked surprised by her quick response. "Do you miss being married?"

It was another question she hadn't expected. "Sometimes," she admitted and took a sip from the mug in her hands. "I miss having someone to talk to. I miss…intimacy."

"Sex?"

Marissa let out a brittle laugh to hide the discomfort climbing across her skin. "Now, that's a typically male response to the idea of intimacy."

"We're not very complex creatures," he said and smiled. "But I do know the difference between emotional and physical intimacy."

"Glad to hear it."

She meant to sound flippant, humorous. But once her words were out they sounded altogether different. Almost like a flirtation…or an invitation. His eyes darkened and he placed the mug on the table. Marissa held his gaze, even though her heart was pounding and all she wanted to do was run for her life.

"You know," he said quietly, his deep voice the only sound she heard, "you really are incredibly beautiful."

Her breath sharpened. "Don't."

His brows rose. "Don't what?"

"Don't flirt with me."

Grady's eyes were suddenly even a more brilliant blue. "Is that what I'm doing?"

"I don't know what you're doing."

He laughed softly. "Frankly, neither do I, Marissa. But there's something about you that's impossible to ignore."

"You mean the fact we've always disliked one another?"

"I've never disliked you."

Her insides folded like origami paper. "But you hardly ever talk to me."

"We're talking now," he reminded her.

"I mean before," she said quickly. "When Liz was alive. I thought you only ever put up with me because I was Liz's friend."

He shrugged loosely, as if she'd made a point he didn't quite want to admit. "I…like you."

He didn't sound as if he did. It sounded as though it was one of the hardest things he'd ever said. She bit back the urge to tell him the feeling was mutual. But she didn't want any more regrettable words hanging in the air between them.

"I should go," she said, scraping the chair back as she stood.

Grady got to his feet immediately and didn't try to stop her. Marissa grabbed her bag, thanked him for the coffee and walked down the hallway. He was beside her in a flash, opening the front door wide as they both stepped out onto the porch.

"Thank you for coming, I know it meant a lot to the girls."

She nodded. "Me, too. Good night."

"Good night," he said and then called her name when she was almost at the bottom of the steps.

"Yes?"

He took his time. "I like you enough that I wanted to ask you to prom in senior year."

Prom? What was he talking about? She shook her head. "You asked Liz."

He nodded. "I wanted to ask you first. She talked me out of it. She said you weren't interested."

Oh, Liz.

Marissa pushed back her shoulders, fighting the denial sitting on the edge of her tongue. "I guess she knew me better than I thought. Good night, Grady."

By the time she got to her car, her hands were shaking. They were still shaking five minutes later when she arrived home, and still as she peeled off her clothes and changed into comfy sweats. She was shaking and thinking one thing.

Liz had lied.

In the middle of senior year she'd confided to her best friend that she was crushing on Grady just a little and hoped he'd ask her to prom. He didn't. Instead he'd asked Liz and after that they were very much a couple. Liz had assured her she wouldn't date Grady if Marissa found it hard to deal with—but she couldn't deny her friend the happiness she deserved. Liz blossomed as she fell in love with Grady, so Marissa tucked away her silly schoolgirl crush, never mentioned it again and got on with being Liz's best friend. And she *did* get over it. She went to college, got her MBA and worked her way into a great job. Then she met Simon and had been happy…until it all fell apart. Through those years, she'd stayed loyal to her friend—through Liz's fairy-tale wedding to Grady, to the first time she'd announced she was having his baby and then when Breanna was born.

And she'd never harbored one ounce of envy or resentment. She'd loved Liz and had been heartbroken when she'd died. And she wouldn't let the knowledge of something that happened so many years ago taint her memories.

Still, she slipped into bed with a heavy heart and woke up around six. She ate breakfast and changed into some yard clothes, fully intent on spending the morning outside weeding and pruning. Rex arrived just before nine and she spent a few minutes showing him the broken palings and then left him to his own devices. He was a quiet man and barely made eye contact with her.

Around nine-thirty, Marissa was around the side of the house pulling out the remnants of an old vegetable patch when she heard a vehicle pull up to the house. She got to her feet, dropped the gardening gloves and wiped her hands down her jeans before going to investigate.

Grady's truck and horse trailer was parked in the driveway and he was hanging around the back end of the vehicle. She spotted Rex coming around from the backyard and the two men spoke for a moment before the trailer door was opened and the ramp came down. Less than a minute later Grady was leading a dark-colored horse off the ramp and across her driveway.

She walked toward him and planted her hands on her hips. "What's this?"

He held out the lead. "For you."

"What?"

"She needs a home," he said and looked around at the pasture and stables adjoining the house yard. "And you have room."

Marissa continued to stare at him. "You're giving me a horse?" she asked and noticed Rex was by the rear of the truck, watching their exchange with a kind of wary interest.

Grady shrugged. "She's old, around twenty-six. But

she's in good health and will do for a riding horse until you are confident in the saddle."

Marissa stroked the mare's cheek. "Where did she come from?"

"I picked her up from the sale yards a few years ago. The girls learned how to handle a horse with this old mare. She was too big for them as a riding pony, but she'll be okay for you."

The mare rubbed her face affectionately against Marissa's arm. "She's just lovely. But I'll pay you for her."

"No need," he said and began to walk the horse toward the neighboring paddock. "She's more than earned her semiretirement."

Marissa followed and waited by the fence while he turned the old mare out into the pasture. He did everything with such a natural ease she couldn't help but admire him. The mare whinnied when she was released and trotted around for a few minutes, tail and head extended.

"She's just beautiful. Thank you…it's very generous of you."

Grady rested his elbows on the fence and turned his head toward her. "I thought you'd like the company."

"I do," she said and smiled. "But won't the girls miss her?"

"They have their own ponies. Old Ebony hasn't been getting a lot of attention of late."

"I'll see that she does," Marissa said. "I'll need to get some gear—like a saddle and bridle."

"No need," Grady replied. "Rex is unloading some gear into the stables for you."

"Thank you," she said and managed a small smile. "But I really… I have to…"

"It's a gift, Marissa," he said and straightened. "But if

that's too hard for you to accept, consider it an exchange for your kindness toward my daughters."

"I don't need payment to love the girls, Grady. Really, what kind of person do you take me for?"

He made an exasperated sound and she felt his rising anger. Unease snaked down her spine. But this wasn't Simon. She had nothing to fear from Grady. She knew that. It was herself she feared. And the feelings running riot throughout her body.

"Can I ever get anything right with you? I wasn't criticizing. I wasn't inferring anything. Maybe I just wanted to give you a horse because you said you wanted to learn to ride. Maybe I just wanted to do something nice for you, Marissa."

"Why?"

Grady's expression suddenly looked like thunder and she winced. "Who the hell knows!"

Then he took off back to his truck and reversed out of the driveway as if he had the devil on his tail.

Chapter Four

"You got somethin' on your mind you want to talk about?"

Grady hauled another hay bale from the truck and twisted around. Rex Travers was standing behind him, arms crossed, his weathered face wrinkled in a scowl. He liked Rex—the other man was a good foreman and had become an important part of the running of the ranch. Grady also considered him a friend. The girls adored him and he was genuinely kind and patient with them. But he wasn't about to get drawn into a conversation about his bad mood.

"Not a thing," Grady replied and tossed the bale onto the stack in the feed shed.

"You took off from Miss Violet's place in a real hurry this morning."

I took off from Marissa...

Grady grabbed another bale. "And?"

"And you yelled at Miss Ellis."

Miss Violet. Miss Ellis. When it came to women, Rex was a stickler for formality. He still referred to Grady's mom as Mrs. Parker even though she'd been insisting the other man call her Colleen for many years.

"I didn't yell," Grady shot back, irritated.

Rex's thick brows came up. "Yeah, you did. She didn't like it."

Grady stopped what he was doing and straightened. "She said that?"

Rex shrugged. "She didn't say anything. I just got a look at her face, that's all. I don't think she likes yelling."

"I didn't yell," Grady said again and wiped his hands down his jeans. "Can we get back to work now? I want you to take Pete and head down to Flat Rock this afternoon. There's a length of fence that needs repairing down by the riverbed, where we butt the McCord place."

"Sure," Rex said. "Anything else?"

"Stop dishing out advice."

Rex's craggy face creased in a wide smile. "Can't promise anything."

"Try harder," Grady said and grabbed another hay bale.

The older man chuckled as he walked off, and when he was out of sight Grady stopped what he was doing, straightened and rolled his shoulders. Damn…he hated it when Rex was right. It felt as bad as being told off by his mother. And he *really* hated that, thinking it made him feel about fifteen years old.

He finished stacking the hay and headed back to the house. His mother was in the kitchen making lunch for Tina. Since his housekeeper had left, his mom had been helping out with the girls. Once he'd washed up in the mudroom, he headed for the kitchen.

"Thanks for coming over today," he said, swiping a slice of cheese off the plate and popping it in his mouth. "I appreciate it."

"Anytime," his mother replied. "You know the girls

mean the world to me. But you remember that I'm heading out of town on Thursday and won't be back for five days."

His mother went to visit her brother in Denver, Colorado, once a year.

"I remember," he said and moved around the counter. "Brant said he'd help out if I needed him. Plus, Tanner and Cassie always love having the girls. And Brooke will always help out if I need a sitter."

Brooke Laughton was his cousin and owned a small horse ranch not far out of town.

"Any luck looking for a new housekeeper?"

He shrugged. "I have two interviews next week, so we'll see what happens."

His mother nodded and continued slicing cheese. "You know…what you really need isn't a housekeeper," she said and smiled. "It's a wife."

"Mom, let up, will you?"

"It's the truth," she said, as relentless as always. "I know you don't want to hear it and you can scowl at me all you like, but I—"

"I'm not scowling," he said, cutting her off.

His mother grinned. "Oh, yes, you are. But you know, the best thing for the girls would be for you to be happy."

"I am happy. And I don't want to have this conversation today."

"Or any day," Colleen said. "Liz wouldn't want you to—"

"Mom," Grady said, all out of patience. "I know you're trying to help, but I'm *fine*," he insisted. "I'm not going to get married again just so I can have a babysitter on hand."

"I'm not suggesting that you should do that," his mother replied. "This isn't about the girls. I'm talking about *you*, what it would mean to you to share your life with someone.

All I'm saying is that maybe it's time you opened yourself up to the possibility."

"Like you did after Dad died?"

Colleen frowned. "I didn't have three children under the age of seven," she reminded him. "And we aren't talking about me at the moment. I know you don't want to hear it and I know you think I'm interfering, but I only say this out of concern for you. Being with someone else doesn't mean you love Liz any less. It doesn't mean she'll be replaced or forgotten."

Grady swallowed the thickness in his throat. As usual, his mom was getting into his head. "I know... I just don't think I'm ready."

"To love again?"

"To *feel* again."

Colleen smiled and patted his arm. "But that's what makes us human, son."

"Maybe. And I hear what you're saying. But I have to do this in my own way."

She tutted. "The *slow* way. You're so much like your father. He also overthought *everything*. Did you know it took him eight months to ask me out on a date?"

Grady glanced at his mother and groaned. "Is there a point to this conversation?"

"Of course," she replied and grinned. "You're a cowboy and it's time you got back in the saddle."

"The saddle?"

His mother smiled. "Yes, you know, dating and girls."

He laughed loudly. "Oh, we're gonna have *that* talk," he said and shrugged. "Too late, Mom, I already know about the birds and the bees."

Colleen jabbed him with her elbow. "You can mock me all you like. Just don't dismiss the idea of dating again entirely, okay?"

"I won't," he assured her. "If you'll stop hinting about who I should date."

She made a face and then nodded. "Sure. These are ready," she said and pushed a plate of sandwiches across the counter. "I'll go and get the baby so she can have her lunch." His mother headed for the door, just as Grady was pulling plates from the cupboard. "By the way, have you seen Marissa lately?"

Grady stilled at the task and groaned inwardly. There was no point lying to Colleen Parker; she'd sniff out an untruth at fifty paces. "I dropped Ebony off there this morning," he explained as casually as he could. "You know, the old black mare."

Colleen's inquisitive brows shot up. "You gave her a horse? That was nice of you."

He shrugged. "She wants to learn to ride and the mare was just—"

"You don't have to explain your reasons," his mother said, grinning in a cat-that-got-the-canary kind of way. "I like Marissa. She's kind and considerate and the girls obviously adore her, so I'm pleased you are both getting along."

We're not...

But he wasn't going to tell her that. He knew what was going on in his mom's head. She was matchmaking. She thought Marissa to be the ideal candidate in her plans to see him married again, and she was not being too subtle about it, either. But it was out of the question. No matter how many times he'd let it shift around in his head over the past couple of days, it always gave him the same feeling. The same unease. The same guilt.

Still, he didn't like thinking that he'd yelled at Marissa.

"Can you watch Tina for an hour before I head into town to pick the girls up from school?" he asked his mother. "I need to run an errand."

Colleen grinned. "You're going to see Marissa?"

Grady shrugged lightly. "Don't get the wrong idea."

"I never do. You know, sometimes what you need isn't necessarily what you think you want. Or don't want."

He frowned. "I have no idea what that means."

She grinned wider. "Oh, I think you do."

He ignored the gleam in his mother's eyes and headed out.

It took barely ten minutes to get to Miss Violet's house. He didn't want to think about the place being Marissa's. That meant permanence. Sure, she'd said she was back for good, but he figured there was too much city girl in her to turn her back on her former life forever.

Grady pulled up outside the cottage and got out of the truck. He could hear music, something loud and modern. He headed up the steps and knocked on the door. No answer. He gave up and walked around the porch to the rear of the house. Marissa was in the garden, kneeling by an overgrown flower bed. Probably the same one Earl had been grazing on a few days earlier. She wore jeans and a plaid shirt tied at her waist and her hair was hidden beneath a floppy straw hat. He watched as she dug the weeds out with a small three-pronged fork and swayed her hips in time to the blaring music. His blood spiked instantly and he shook the feeling off. He didn't want to be stirred by Marissa. He didn't want to think about her curves or warm chocolate eyes or soft, lush mouth.

She stopped moving, as though aware she was being observed, and turned on her knees.

Then she dropped the fork and got to her feet. She didn't say a word as she came up the steps and walked into the house through the back door. The music stopped a few seconds later and she came back outside, two bottles of cold soda in her hands. She passed him one and their knuckles grazed.

The touch was enough to heat his skin, and he quickly flipped the top off the bottle to do something with his hands.

The silence between them spoke volumes. It stretched and amplified. It mocked his determination to *not* think about her.

Finally, he spoke. "I'm sorry if I yelled at you this morning."

She rested her hips on the porch railing, tilted the straw hat back and looked at him. "You came all this way to apologize?"

"We only live next door," he reminded her. "And, yes. It was made clear to me that I was something of a jerk this morning."

"Only this morning?" she inquired.

Grady spotted a soil mark on the side of her face. He grabbed the bandanna from his back pocket and stepped closer. "Hold still," he instructed and quickly wiped the mark off. When he was done, he moved back and returned the cloth to his pocket. "That's better."

Her cheeks were pink, her eyes bright, her mouth slightly apart. He couldn't recall her ever looking more beautiful. And in that moment he realized an irrefutable fact. The niggling irritation that had plagued him for days was due to one thing…he was attracted to Marissa. And he suddenly felt as if he was back in high school. Back thinking about taking her to prom. Back being told by Liz that Marissa wasn't interested in him.

He'd loved Liz wholly and completely and had dismissed his teenage attraction for Marissa a long time ago. But now it felt as if it had returned with a vengeance, taunting him, making him feel like the biggest fool of all time.

"So, who's responsible for this revelation of yours?" she asked as she took a sip of soda.

For a moment he wondered if she was reading his

thoughts, but quickly realized what she meant. "Rex, my foreman. He said I yelled at you. He also said you didn't like it."

"He's right on both counts. He's a smart man."

Shame crept up his neck. "I apologize. I didn't mean to upset you. I was—"

"I know," she said, cutting him off. "We always do that to one another."

"It's no excuse for yelling. I'm not that person...generally."

"Only around me, you mean?"

Discomfiture snaked up his spine. "I was mad with myself this morning and I shouldn't have taken that out on you."

She sighed and smiled fractionally. "I probably sounded ungrateful. But I'm not. It was very nice of you to give me Ebony. I spent some time with her this afternoon and she has such a sweet nature."

"Yeah," he said casually. "I thought you two would get along."

She looked at him over the bottle. "Are you saying I'm sweet, too?"

Grady backpedaled. "My mom thinks so."

She smiled. "That's quite an endorsement."

"Yeah, that's my mother. She's likes you. And she appreciates how much you care about her grandchildren."

"I love the girls," she said and took a shallow breath. "And your mom has always been kind to me. She held my hand at Liz's funeral, did you know that? She sat beside me and helped me through the service."

Grady's chest constricted. "Like you helped me in the kitchen once everyone had left?"

She sucked in a sharp breath. "You remember that?"

"Of course," he replied. "As for my mom, no, I didn't know that."

"I think she must have realized how alone I felt without much family…and knowing how much I cared about Liz. I'll always be grateful for her support that day."

It sounded like something his mother would do. "She's a good person."

Marissa nodded. "You're lucky to have her."

"I know," he said and smiled ruefully. "Even if she's on a mission at the moment."

"A mission?"

"To see me…you know…with someone."

She grinned. "You mean married?"

"Precisely."

"And is that what you want?" she asked.

Grady drank some soda and shrugged loosely. "I don't know."

"Because you still feel married to Liz?"

It was the first time anyone had asked him the question he figured should have seemed obvious. But Marissa seemed to get it. And she wasn't worried about asking. Then again, she'd been there from the beginning…from their wedding to each of the girls being born and then when Liz had died. Marissa probably knew his feelings better than anyone because she'd also loved Liz. It was a bond they would always share. One that drew them together as much as it pulled them apart.

"People can't just turn off feelings."

She stared at him, her eyes wide. "You're right about that."

He wondered if she was thinking about her ex-husband. She'd said she didn't love him now, but Grady wasn't entirely convinced. It would certainly explain the lost, almost haunted look in her eyes at times. He didn't like how the notion rattled him. "So, am I forgiven?"

She nodded. "Sure. Liz wouldn't want us to be at odds with one another."

"That's true. Your friendship was very important to her. And it is to me, too, Marissa. Liz knew..." His words trailed off for a moment. "She knew how important you would be to the girls once she was gone."

He met her gaze and saw the shine in her eyes. "I'll always be there for them."

"I know."

Liz had known it, too. There were two things she'd asked of him before she died—to keep Marissa in their lives and for him to be happy.

They were Liz's last words. And he'd made a promise that day. A promise he hadn't quite fulfilled. Because he was content, not happy. He had his kids, his ranch, his family and friends... He had a lot to be grateful for. Expecting more seemed churlish. Greedy. Arrogant.

"Well...I should get going and let you return to your gardening."

"Sure. Actually, I'm heading off to see Aunt Violet soon."

Grady nodded. "How long before she comes home?"

Marissa lifted one shoulder. "*If* she comes home. She's talking about moving into a retirement complex, like those new ones near the hospice where your uncle lives."

Grady's uncle Joe had lived at the Veterans home for a number of years, and the newly developed retirement complex was a couple of blocks down the street. "Will you stay here if she does?"

"I told you I was back for good. And I could buy this place off Aunt Violet. I have enough in savings and from my divorce settlement. All those greenhouses my great-uncle built years ago are going to waste, so I could try my hand at growing organic vegetables."

Marissa Ellis as a farmer? Not what he expected to hear. "Do you know anything about organic vegetables?"

"Not a thing," she replied. "But since there's little call for New York marketing executives in Cedar River, and I have to do something, I thought it might be worth looking into. Besides, I'm a fast learner."

Grady didn't doubt that. "I hope it works out for you."

She groaned. "Honestly, Grady, sometimes you can be so condescending."

"Part of my charm," he said and grinned. "But what about turning one of them into a studio?"

She stilled. "I don't know. I haven't touched a pottery wheel for years."

Grady knew that. She'd left for college on an art scholarship and switched majors after two terms. Liz said she'd wanted something more reliable than the dream of opening up her own store to showcase her wares.

"Maybe it's time to pick it back up? There are several gift stores in town now that cater to the tourists. Those fancy mugs you used to make would probably go over really well with that crowd."

She shrugged. "Maybe."

"And speaking of learning new things, you get your first riding lesson on Saturday morning. I'll let you know what time."

Her expression brightened. "Oh, okay."

"I'd better be off. I have to pick Breanna and Milly up from school." He propped the empty soda bottle on the small table by the door, then looked at her. "You can drop by and see the girls anytime. You know that, right?"

"I know," she said and nodded. "Goodbye, Grady."

He tilted his hat and walked around the porch.

But damn if he couldn't help thinking that he wanted to

stay and talk with her just a little longer. And that, he fig-ured as he drove off, meant he was in deep, serious trouble.

People can't just turn off feelings...

Marissa was thinking about Grady's confession for days afterward.

And wondering why he'd come to see her when a tele-phone call would have sufficed. It wasn't as if they were friends...not really. They were connected because of Liz. They both knew that. She was pleased they'd cleared the air, but his suggestion about setting up a studio had made her think about what she'd given up. Marissa had aban-doned her dreams of making a living from her craft a long time ago. She'd studied business and marketing and pot-ted only as a hobby. Then she met Simon and her hobby became a distant memory. Toward the end of their mar-riage and in one of his rages he'd smashed most of her pieces, and since then she'd lost the urge to create and get her hands into the clay.

But maybe Grady was right. Maybe one of the green-houses would make an ideal studio.

The week flew by, with several visits to Aunt Violet, who confirmed that she'd decided to stay in town after her rehab. She gave Marissa the opportunity to buy the small ranch. She had planned on living with Aunt Violet, and certainly had enough money from her savings and the di-vorce settlement to buy the place outright, and invest some significant dollars into the farm. But she wasn't sure. She needed time to think about what she truly wanted to do now that she was back.

On Thursday afternoon she returned home around five o'clock and was just about to start packing some of her aunt's things into boxes when her cell rang.

It was Grady.

"Marissa," he said quickly, his voice raspier than usual. "My brother has been in an accident and I need to get to the hospital. My mother is out of town and I was wondering if you would be able to watch the girls for me."

"Of course. I'll be right there."

Twelve minutes later she pulled up outside Grady's ranch house. He was on the porch, pacing, car keys in his hand. He took the steps and met her by her Volvo.

"Thank you," he said and sighed heavily. "Rex is out mending fences. Otherwise I would have asked him."

Marissa clutched his arm. "Is your brother seriously hurt?"

He shrugged and tapped her hand. "I'm not sure. The hospital called to say he fell off his motorbike. I'll ring you when I know more. Breanna and Milly are in their rooms reading and Tina is playing in the nursery."

"You go," she said and ushered him off. "We'll be fine."

By the time Marissa grabbed her tote and climbed the steps, all she could see was the dust from the wheels of his pickup. She headed inside and checked in on Tina. The littlest Parker was playing with blocks in her room and was instantly distracted when Marissa walked across the threshold. Tina was in her arms in seconds and she walked up the hall to see the older girls. Breanna and Milly were clearly delighted to see her, and she sat with them for a few minutes while they read from their books in turn. Once they'd finished, she settled Tina in the playpen and then made her way to the kitchen to make coffee.

The huge kitchen was in the center of the house and overlooked the pool and gardens. Marissa could recall the countless times she'd sat with Liz at the huge square table, sharing coffee and conversation and dreams for the future. It was where her friend had told her she was expecting her first baby, and Marissa remembered it as if it was yesterday.

Liz had been so happy that day. Glowing and in love with Grady and filled with happiness.

She sighed heavily. She missed her friend. She missed having someone to talk to, to confide in. Sure, she'd had friends in New York, but none whom she trusted enough to share her innermost thoughts. When she'd learned about Simon's infidelity, she'd longed for her friend. When her ex-husband had repeatedly yelled at her and called her boring and cold and as passionless as an ice cube, she'd wished she had someone to tell. And on that last day, when Simon had been so enraged he'd struck her and grabbed her by the throat, she'd gone to the police alone, so ashamed that she hadn't been able to see the man she believed she'd loved for what he was—a violent, womanizing brute. Of course, the charges hadn't stuck. Simon was too influential, too charming. But she'd tried to defend herself and sought some comfort in that.

But told no one. Not even Aunt Violet. Over the past twelve months, she'd longed for a family more than ever before. For brothers and sisters. For a mother. For a dad. Someone who could be her champion. But there was no one. So, after living alone for a year, when Grady had called to say her aunt needed her, she'd finally packed up her life and headed home.

Marissa took a deep, steadying breath and made coffee, then looked through the refrigerator and considered what she could give the girls for dinner. She found a casserole in the freezer, considered how long it would take to defrost and then decided on toasted cheese sandwiches.

Rex tapped on the back door half an hour later and walked into the kitchen, hat in his hands. "Evening, Miss Ellis," he said quietly.

"Please, call me Marissa," she insisted. "Did Grady get a hold of you?"

"Yes. I was down at Flat Rock with Pete for most of the afternoon and don't get good cell reception there. But he left a message." He shifted on his feet. "Is there anything you need, Miss Ellis?"

"Marissa," she said again and smiled. There was a kindness about Rex that put her at ease. He wasn't as old as he looked, she was sure. Maybe midfifties. His face was weathered, as if he'd spent one too many summers out in the sun, but he was still quite handsome. And there was something about his brown eyes…something that told her he was a man of deep integrity. "And I'm fine. But thank you for checking, I appreciate it."

His cheeks immediately flushed. "No problem, ma'am… I mean, Marissa."

The way he said her name gave her an unexpected comfort. "Would you like to stay for dinner?"

"No," he said quickly. "I've still got a couple of horses to bed down. Take care, ma'am."

He left as quietly as he'd arrived and Marissa returned to the meal she was preparing. By the time she was done, Tina was ready for her bath and the older girls had their pajamas ready. Once all the kids were bathed and changed, Marissa ushered everyone to the kitchen.

Dinner was a fun affair with lots of spillage and laughter. Afterward she got the girls to brush their teeth and allowed them to watch television for an hour before she put them to bed with another story. Tina stayed up a little later, curled up with Marissa on the sofa in the lounge room. She fell asleep around eight, and Marissa was just contemplating putting the toddler back in her room when she got a text from Grady saying he would soon be on his way home.

As she snuggled Tina, Marissa was overwhelmed by the sense of love she had for the child. *Grady's child.* No…*Liz's* child. In that moment she wasn't sure which made her love the little girl more.

Grady was home half an hour later, and by then Tina was tucked in her bed and the older girls were fast asleep. She put more coffee on and waited for him to walk into the kitchen.

"Well?" she asked and pushed a mug across the counter.

"Brant's okay," Grady said and ran a hand through his already ruffled hair. "He was lucky. He's got a concussion, a dislocated shoulder and some cuts and bruises and is staying overnight. Thank God he had his helmet on."

"That's good news. You must be relieved."

"Yeah," he said and grabbed the mug. "Brant has been through a lot. He survived three tours with the army and saw some pretty scary stuff in the Middle East, so I'd hate to think he made it home and then got seriously hurt or worse on that damned motorbike." He gulped some coffee and let out a long sigh. "Thanks for this. And for watching over the girls."

"It was my pleasure. We had a lovely evening reading and watching TV." She thought how tired he looked. "Have you eaten? If not, why don't you hit the shower and I'll make you something."

Grady nodded. "That would be great, thanks."

He left the room and Marissa made swift work of a BLT sandwich on sourdough bread and put on a fresh pot of coffee. By the time he returned, he looked refreshed and clean in low-riding jeans and a white T-shirt. His feet were bare and it seemed oddly intimate somehow. It was the second time in a week she'd been in his house, his kitchen, his space, and Marissa wondered why she didn't feel more uneasy. Normally she was on red alert when around Grady. But tonight, there was no unease. Even though he looked too gorgeous for words. The T-shirt stretched over his shoulders and across his flat stomach. His damp hair flopped over his forehead in a way that was boyish yet failed to hide the finely chiseled brow or the deep blue of his eyes.

Yes, Grady Parker did sexy without even realizing it!

"Thanks," he said as he sat at the counter. "Everything okay here?"

Marissa nodded. "Kids are all bathed, fed and now in bed. And Rex checked in, which was good of him."

Grady wrapped his hands around his mug and smiled. "He's something of a fan of yours, I think."

"I like him, too. He's very polite and sweet."

Grady laughed. "Sweet? I'll have to tell him that. Most days he's an ornery old cuss. But he's good at his job and like part of the family now."

Marissa sighed. "Yeah…family is important."

Grady looked at her. It was one of those deep, impossibly intense gazes of his that she couldn't break free from, even though she knew she should. "You miss your mom?"

She nodded. "Yes. She did her best raising me on my own. It couldn't have been easy."

Grady's gaze softened. "Have you ever thought of trying to find your father?"

She shrugged. "No point. I don't know anything about him. His name or where he's from. My mother would never tell me. She said it didn't matter. So I can only assume I'm better off *not* knowing, if that makes sense."

He sighed. "You know, you're part of this family, too… You always have been. Even though Liz is gone." His mouth creased in a gentle smile. "And even though we sometimes have a slight communication problem, you're very much a part of things here."

Emotion clutched her throat. Grady being sentimental was a new experience for her. And she wasn't about to admit how much she liked it. Not to him. And certainly not to herself.

"Thanks."

"I know you've probably felt alone since Liz died," he said quietly. "And with your marriage breaking up and now that Miss Violet is getting older, it's understandable that—"

"Are you trying to make me cry?"

"What?" he asked, looking genuinely surprised. "Of course not."

Heat burned the back of her eyes. "Then stop being so nice to me."

He slammed his fist onto the counter. "Damned if I do. Damned if I don't."

She came around the counter and placed the sandwich on the table. "I guess so."

He laughed softly. "You're kidding me, right? Maybe there's a middle road?"

"There probably is," she said. "We just never seem to have been able to find it."

"We've found it now," he shot back. "I'm being nice. You're being nice. See, it's easier than you think."

Nothing was easy when it came to Grady. "I guess I'm not very good at trusting people these days."

He took a bite of the sandwich and then rested back in the chair. "I meant what I said—I would never intentionally make you cry. Or hurt you. That's not the kind of man I am."

Marissa's throat choked up. There was such absolute honesty in his words. There was nothing mean or cruel about Grady. He was strong and confident. He was the polar opposite of her ex-husband. He would never physically hurt her or any woman. He had integrity. A code of honor that was ingrained within him. He could be trusted. And just when she'd convinced herself she'd never trust a man again, Marissa realized that she had done exactly that. In that moment she felt more vulnerable, more naked and more visible than she ever remembered feeling before.

And she couldn't have stopped the tears in her eyes even if she'd wanted to.

Chapter Five

Grady was up and out of his seat in a microsecond. He reached out and grasped Marissa's shoulders, looking down at her. The tears tipped over her lids and ran down her cheeks as her shoulders shook.

"What?" he asked softly, steadying her so she wouldn't fall. "Marissa, what is it? Tell me."

She met his gaze and the despair in her brown eyes cut through him. "Oh, Grady… I can't…"

Grady's insides constricted. She'd never spoken his name like that before. On a whisper. On a sigh. And he'd never seen her look more vulnerable. Or more lost. Something was wrong.

"You can. What's going on in that head of yours?" he asked gently. "If I've said something to upset you, I'm sorry. I certainly didn't—"

"No," she said and shook her head. "It's nothing you've done."

"But someone's upset you," he said, too afraid to release

her while she was clearly so emotional. He had another thought. "Was it Rex? Or—"

"No," she refuted quickly. "He didn't upset me. He's a nice man. It's me… I guess I'm not as strong as I used to be. So much has happened and I think I'm simply tired and worn-out."

Grady didn't quite believe her. There was something in her expression…anxiety…fear. Strange, but he'd never thought Marissa to be afraid of anything. She was always in control. Always self-assured. But the woman in front of him was not the Marissa he believed he knew. She'd come home different. Changed. Something had happened to her… And then it occurred to him, as if he'd been hit with a freight train, and he realized he should have worked it out sooner. One question instantly burned inside Grady.

One question he didn't want to ask but was compelled to.

"Marissa…what did he do to you?"

She stilled instantly and pulled back, putting space between them. Grady dropped his hands and looked at her. And in that moment he was sure…certain that his suspicions were correct.

"Nothing."

"You're lying," Grady said quietly, watching as she stepped back again. "You're lying to protect him."

Fresh tears filled her eyes, but she remained silent. Tension stretched between them and Grady pushed back the rising anger fueling his blood. Because he should have known, he should have figured that something important had brought her back to Cedar River. And not just her aunt's accident.

He'd never liked Simon Burke. He'd never trusted the other man or thought he was worth a lick of anything. He rallied himself to ask another question, one that made him sick to the stomach.

"He hurt you, didn't he?"

His words hung in the air, but finally, after what seemed like minutes, she nodded. It seemed to take all her strength. All her resolve. And then she sagged like a rag doll. Moving quickly, Grady hauled her into his arms, enfolding her gently. She didn't resist. Didn't do anything other than wilt against him. He smoothed her hair with one hand and held on to her waist with the other.

She stayed like that for several minutes. When she finally pulled back, she looked relieved, as if some great burden had been lifted from her shoulders. Grady remained where he was until she sat down and then pulled a chair out and sat beside her. He resisted the urge to hold her hand and waited…waited until she took a breath and spoke.

"He hit me," she admitted quietly. "That last day."

Rage rose upward in his chest, but Grady pushed it back down. He had more questions. He wanted more answers. "Had he done it before?"

She shook her head fractionally. "He'd been verbally abusive for a while…even before I found out about the affairs. But on the day I left, the day I told him I was leaving and wanted a divorce, he was angrier than usual…he yelled more than usual. He said he wouldn't give me an easy divorce, and then he slapped me hard a couple of times." She pointed to her cheek. "Right here. And then grabbed me and put his hands around my throat and started to…" Her words trailed off and she drew in a shuddering breath. "He started to choke me. I think he just wanted to scare me…which he did."

Grady's hands fisted in his lap as a turbulent, gathering rage whirled through his system and rooted deep into his blood and bones. He usually deplored violence, but if Simon Burke had been in the vicinity he would have happily punched him in the face.

"You got away, though?"

She nodded. "I think he realized what he was doing and he released me. Not before he hit me again. And again. And then he went to the kitchen and smashed all the mugs…you know, the ones I'd made over the years. He left one on the shelf… I always thought that strange…like he was making a statement about still controlling me." She sighed heavily. "Anyway, I moved out that day and checked into a hotel."

"Did you call the police?"

"I filed a complaint," she said and sighed again. "But Simon hired this whiz-bang lawyer and the case was thrown out."

Grady's rage returned. "What happened then?"

"Simon was my boss, so he saw to it that I lost my job and also that I wouldn't get another in the same industry. I quickly became Madison Avenue poison and after a few months realized I was never going to be able to continue with my career. So I leased an apartment and did some temp work for a few more months. And then Aunt Violet had her accident, so I came back to Cedar River…divorced, out of a job, out of options."

Grady grasped her hand. It was small and easily fit inside his. Her skin was soft and he gripped her fingers gently. "I know you already know this, Marissa, but not all men hit. Most of us spend our life knowing it's our job to protect the women we care about."

"And even the ones you don't?" she asked tremulously.

Grady frowned. "Is that what you think? That I don't care about you?" He squeezed her hand. "Of course I care, Marissa. And if you'd called me, if you'd reached out and said you needed help, I would have come to you. I would have gotten you out of there."

Tears filled her eyes again. "I know you would have. And thank you for saying that," she said on a sigh. "Unfortunately my ex-husband doesn't possess that same moral compass as you."

Grady kept her hand within his. "He was never worthy of you, Marissa. And I think over time you'll come to know that."

"You're right," she said and looked to where their hands were linked. "Thank you for listening. For understanding. I haven't ever told anyone what happened. I was too... ashamed."

Grady frowned. "Of what? Being married to a jerk?"

"Of not seeing him for who he was. *What* he was. I married a man I hardly knew. My boss, no less. A man with no scruples in business. So I should have known better."

Her pain was palpable, and it cut Grady down deep. "You don't still love him, do you?"

"No," she replied quickly. "Of course not."

He rubbed her palm. "Then you're free, Marissa. Free of him. Free of the past."

Grady reached up and touched her cheek, gently wiping at the tears on her face. She didn't move. Didn't breathe. The moment was incredibly intimate, and as much as he tried to fight what was going on in his head, it felt like a prelude to something.

Like a kiss...

Grady looked at her mouth, saw her lips tremble and knew she was thinking the same thing. He could have kissed her then... He could have moved forward and captured her mouth with his own. He wanted to. Longed to. Part of him needed it as he needed air in his lungs. He could have tasted her lips and drawn her tongue into his mouth. But it would mean too much. Change too much. It would make him *feel* again, when feeling was the last thing he wanted.

"I'll get Rex to follow you home," he said, dropping his hand as he released her and stood.

She remained where she was, breathing heavily, looking at him with widened eyes.

"There's no need for—"

"There's every need," he said, cutting her off.

"Okay," she said quietly. "Thank you."

He watched as she collected her things and pulled keys from her bag. Grady called Rex and asked him to get her home safely, and within minutes she was gone. Out of his house. Out of his life.

Who am I kidding?

Every day, every moment, every second that he spent with Marissa drew them closer together. As long as they spent time with each other they would always be pulled closer. It felt…inevitable. As if some great force had aligned to suddenly make him see the truth that had been glaring at him all week. That he wanted her. In his arms.

In his bed.

I need to stay away from her...

Which wasn't going to happen. Not with the girls, his mom and fate playing their hands.

I need to get control over this...

And that, he figured as he prepared to take the coldest shower in history, wasn't going to happen, either.

I almost kissed Grady last night.

Marissa was still thinking about it as she drove into town late Friday morning. She had shopping to do, a visit with Aunt Violet planned and a promise to meet Rex back at her cottage around two so he could help her move the broken pieces of an old cart wheel that was dredged deeply into one of the flower beds. He'd offered to help the night before when he'd walked her to her door, and Marissa had been touched by his chivalry.

Aunt Violet was in good spirits when she arrived. Her aunt was out of bed and sitting on a chair by the window, her leg propped up in a moon boot. Marissa gave her a hug and sat in the chair opposite.

"How are you?" she asked, noticing her aunt's perky expression. At eighty-two, Violet was silver-haired and plump, and always wore a beaming smile. Marissa loved her dearly and was delighted to see how she'd bounced back from her accident.

"Fighting fit," Violet said and tapped her leg. "Be happier when I get this off so I can start playing croquet again."

"Three more weeks," Marissa reminded her and held up three fingers. "That's what the doctor said."

Violet nodded and smiled. "So, have you started packing up my things? There's three weeks' worth of work for you. Keep whatever furniture you want," Violet said, her eyes twinkling. "I've decided to buy new things for my new home. I've got some brochures here for you to look at." She sighed and passed Marissa a leaflet. "Dreamscape Villas…doesn't that sound fancy?"

Marissa flicked through the pages. "It certainly does. It looks lovely. And I've decided to start in the yard first and then tackle the house. Rex is coming over this afternoon to help me move the—"

"Rex Travers?" Violet asked quickly, cutting her off. "Grady's foreman?"

Marissa nodded. "Yes, that's him."

Violet's brown eyes darkened a little, as if she disapproved. But she couldn't possibly disapprove of Rex. Her aunt's expression shifted quickly and she smiled. "That's very neighborly of him. So," she said stiffly, changing the subject, "when are you bringing those adorable girls back to visit me?"

"I'll ask Grady," Marissa replied and ignored the way her skin heated by simply saying his name.

I almost kissed Grady last night...

There it was again. Swirling around in her head. In a moment of madness, when she was touched by his kindness and understanding and had felt the strength of his arms around her, she'd been tempted...sorely tempted to press closer and feel his mouth on hers. He'd been thinking it, too, she was sure of it. Desire had thrummed through the air, creating a kind of crazy alchemy of the senses.

And if they had kissed? What then?

Would it have meant anything? Or everything? One thing she knew for sure—they could never have gone back to being what they were.

Which is what, exactly?

Not really friends. But more than acquaintances. Linked together forever because of Liz. Two people in each other's lives only because of three little girls they both loved. And what of the future? What if Grady remarried? How would she feel about Marissa's role in their lives? Not an aunt... not really anything...just someone who'd made a promise to a dying woman.

And what would Liz make of her behavior the night before? The comfort and safety she'd felt in Grady's arms was unlike anything she'd known before. And it terrified her.

"Marissa?"

Aunt Violet's voice pulled her thoughts back to the present. "I'll ask Grady when I can bring them for another visit. I'm sure he won't mind."

Violet nodded. "Such a tragedy what happened to him and those girls. But he's done a good job raising them alone.

Although Colleen Parker thinks he should look at settling down again. Those girls need a mother and—"

"Some single parents do just fine," Marissa said quickly, somehow defending Grady even though it wasn't her intention. "I didn't have a father, and Mom and I managed okay."

Violet offered a gentle smile. "Yes, Janie did her best. She worked at the salon and put a roof over your head. She lost her parents when she was young and I don't think she ever fully recovered. I tried, of course, much like I did with you." Her aunt's eyes shimmered. "But you were an easier child to deal with…not so headstrong and obstinate. Your mother had a way of finding trouble."

"Like when she got pregnant with me at seventeen?"

Violet shrugged. "To her credit, she was determined to raise you herself. And she would have, I'm sure, if she hadn't got sick. In a way it was better that she went quickly."

Janie Ellis was struck down with pancreatic cancer at barely twenty-nine and fought the illness for seven long months before she passed away. "Yes, I suppose. But I would have liked more time to say goodbye. To ask questions."

One question. *Who is my father?* Her mother never spoke of him. And Aunt Violet said she didn't know anything other than he was a drifter, a weekend cowboy passing through town. Over the years Marissa had learned to be content with that answer. But some days she ached to know the truth.

She stayed for another ten minutes and then headed off. She drove to the supermarket and did some shopping, and it was just past two o'clock when she arrived home.

Grady's pickup was parked outside and she figured Rex was already around the back. Marissa grabbed the groceries and headed up the path and onto the porch. She placed the bags on the old swinging love seat and walked around the house. And stopped in her tracks.

Sure enough, Rex was there. But so was Grady. Stripped down to jeans and a white tank shirt that emphasized every contour of his chest. He was standing at one end of the old wagon wheel, levering it with an iron bar, while Rex stayed on the other side and pushed against the wheel. She rested her hand on the railing and felt something soft against her palm. She looked down. Grady's shirt. She fingered the fabric for a moment and let out a soft sigh. It was late summer and a warm day, which explained why he had discarded his shirt. Marissa watched for a moment, riveted by the way his arms flexed and moved and the soft sheen of perspiration on his skin. It took a moment before both men realized they were being observed. Grady stopped what he was doing and turned, resting one elbow on the old wagon wheel.

"Afternoon, ma'am."

It was Rex who spoke. But it was Grady who had her attention. Last night she'd been tempted to kiss this man... and that attraction—as unwanted and out of the question as it was—had not diluted itself overnight.

"What are you doing here?" she asked from her spot on the porch.

Grady wagged a thumb at the broken wagon wheel. "This is a two-man job."

She tried to look grateful but couldn't. And Grady wasn't fooled. There was an intensity in his stare that unnerved her. And he knew it.

"Oh, okay. Well...thanks."

She glanced at Rex and saw how keenly he watched their interaction. Clearly he wasn't fooled, either. She hurried back to the front of the house, grabbed the grocery bags and headed inside. Once the groceries were put away, she poured iced tea, adding way too much sugar to one because she knew Grady liked it that way, and measured half the amount for Rex. By the time she returned outside with the drinks, they had the old wheel and attached axle almost out of the ground.

They stopped what they were doing and took the tumblers she offered. Marissa kept her gaze away from the broad expanse of Grady's chest. It didn't bear thinking about. Not if she wanted to keep her head.

"Thank you, ma'am."

Rex spoke again, looking appreciative, and Marissa smiled. The older man smiled back and she was warmed by his quiet kindness. There was something about the cowboy that she liked, and she remembered her aunt's scowl when they'd talked about him. It was strange, as Aunt Violet seemed to like everyone. But not this man, obviously.

"How's your aunt doin'?" Rex asked, as though reading her thoughts.

Marissa nodded. "Very well," she replied and glanced toward Grady. "She wants to know when I can take the girls to see her again."

Grady passed her the empty glass and their fingertips collided. Her skin burned and she gripped the glass tightly.

"Anytime," he replied and pulled a red bandanna from his back pocket.

"Speaking of the girls, where are they today?"

"Breanna and Milly are in school and my cousin Brooke is watching Tina for an hour."

Marissa had gone to school with Brooke Laughton and knew her reasonably well, even though the other woman had been two grades behind her. Brooke owned a small ranch out of town and was a renowned horsewoman.

She watched as he wiped his face and throat with the cloth. Everything he did had a seductive quality. "Great," she said and took the other glass from Rex. "Thank you both for doing this."

Grady tilted his hat, nodded and got back to work.

Marissa took off as if her heels were on fire. She stayed inside and rearranged one of kitchen cupboards. When that was done, she washed the dishes and cranked up the coffee machine. Grady tapped on the back doorjamb about twenty minutes later and she jumped a little and then turned.

"All done," he said and took off his hat. "We dragged it around to the other side of the fence."

Marissa managed a small smile. "Ah…thank you."

He glanced around the room. "Anything else need doing?"

She shook her head. "No. Thanks again."

Grady remained where he was. "Everything all right, Marissa?"

No…

"Of course."

His mouth turned up at the edges. "You seem a little tense."

She was tense. And they both knew why. She was pretty sure Grady was remembering their *almost* kiss just as she was.

"I'm fine," she lied. "How's your brother?"

"Better," he replied. "They discharged him this morning."

She nodded. "I'm glad to hear it."

"So…Saturday morning?" His brows came up. "Come to the ranch around eight o'clock."

"For what?"

"You said you wanted to learn to ride."

Marissa frowned a little. "I thought I was to learn on Ebony."

"Not the first lesson. You'll be safer in the corral. So, eight o'clock."

She nodded. "Sure. See you then." He turned and walked toward the door and was about to disappear when she called his name. "Thanks again, Grady. For helping Rex move the wagon wheel."

He stilled and turned back. "No problem. You're gathering quite the fan club—first the girls and my mom, now Rex."

She shrugged as casually as she could. "I guess I have a certain kind of charm."

His gaze bored into hers. "Yeah," he said, sounding as if the confession was almost against his will. "You certainly do."

Then he was gone.

On Saturday morning Marissa dressed in her new riding breeches and belt, hot-pink plaid shirt and sparkly cowboy boots she bought from the shoe store in town. The last pair like them, she was told by the clerk in the shop. They were flashy, but Marissa felt she needed a little flashy in her life. She arrived at the Parker ranch at three minutes to eight. Grady was by the main corral, wearing his usual jeans and chambray shirt. Breanna and Milly were chasing one of the dogs around the yard and she spotted Tina in a shaded play area by the stable door. The older girls raced up and hugged her and Marissa held a hand of each as they walked her toward the corral.

Grady looked her over and stopped when he got to her feet. "Interesting boots."

The diamantes on the side of her bright pink boots shimmered in the morning sunlight. "You said to get boots. So I got boots."

"You know that Ron's been trying to palm off the last pair for nearly two years," he said about the owner of the shoe store. "The tourists seemed to like them."

"I'm not a tourist," Marissa reminded him and smiled

extra sweetly. "I'm a local. And luckily I scored the last pair."

"Yeah…that's close to two hundred bucks' worth of luck right there."

"We love them, Daddy!" Milly exclaimed with her usual excitement. "And we want boots just like Marissa's."

He groaned and grinned. "See what you've done? Now I'll be online shopping for tiny pink cowboy boots."

She laughed. "Enough about the boots. You promised me a riding lesson."

Five minutes later she was in the saddle Grady's horse, a mellow-natured paint gelding called Solo, walked easily around the corral under Grady's instruction. Marissa relaxed, grabbed the reins and allowed her body to move with the rhythm of the animal. She spent thirty minutes learning about legs and heels and balance and how to feel the horse through her thighs and seat and then through the reins and the bit. Grady was a patient and calm instructor and she felt completely safe as she walked and then trotted around the corral. The girls encouraged her from the sidelines and at some point Rex joined in.

She had fun. More fun than she'd had in ages. The lesson lasted about forty-five minutes and when she was done Grady stood closely behind her as she propped her right leg over the back of the saddle and swung herself to the ground.

"That was fabulous," she said and patted the gelding on the neck. "I can't wait to start riding Ebony."

"You're something of a natural," Grady said with a grin as he took the reins. "But you're not done yet. You have to untack him and brush him down."

"Oh, okay."

The girls were back playing chase with the dog and Rex had hauled a now-wailing Tina from her play area and was walking her around the yard. Grady led the horse from the corral and through to the stables. The stall was small and clean and covered with a bed of thick straw. He tied the gelding to a hitching ring and instructed her to stand by the horse.

"Unclip this," he said and pointed to the breastplate. "And then this," he said about the girth strap. "Then slide the saddle gently over his back."

Marissa did as he asked and finally slid the saddle and blanket off. He took the gear and balanced it on the top of the stall door. Then he grabbed a brush from a bucket by the door.

"Now take this," he said and placed the brush in her hand. "Don't be afraid to use it. Start at the neck and work downward, along the grain of the coat. Avoid the face and legs and pay particular attention to the girth and just below the withers."

Marissa fumbled with the brush and managed a few short movements. How could she possibly concentrate when Grady was watching her so intently?

"No," he said quietly, coming closer. "Like this."

He stood behind her, his hand over hers, holding the brush, smoothing the coat down in long strokes. His arm brushed against hers, his chest moved against her back. Marissa stilled, unable to move, willing life into her limbs but unable to garner any. The only movement was their hands and arms, traveling down over and over, in perfect unison.

"See," he said, his voice warm and seductive. "Just like this. Long, firm strokes."

Heat rose up between them, circling, teasing…making her long to step back, to get closer and to feel his arms around her. Her skin was on fire. Her breath felt as if it would form flame. And she felt so wired, so aroused, it was frighteningly heady.

"Marissa," he said close to her ear, his breath warm and

intoxicating. "Do you have any idea what you're doing to me?"

"I don't—"

"I almost kissed you the other night," he admitted, his voice raw.

"I know," she whispered.

"I wanted to," he rasped, so close, so softly. "I wanted to so much I ache thinking about it."

She swallowed hard. "I…I wanted it, too."

He moaned softly. "You're killing me, you know that?"

There was anguish in his voice. Anguish and desire. The kind of churning emotions that should have made her run like the wind. But she didn't. Instead, she wanted to turn around. She wanted to press herself against him and be kissed over and over. She wanted to fall down into the bed of straw and make love with him. Over and over. Again and again. Her sex-starved, *love-starved* body suddenly needed him as she needed air to breathe.

But a sound, like someone clearing his throat, quickly pushed them apart.

It was Rex, holding a subdued Tina. He stood by the door and was uncharacteristically glaring at Grady. Marissa took a couple of steps sideways and breathed deeply. The last thing she wanted was to be caught almost making out with Grady in the stables. Particularly when his daughters and foreman were nearby.

"Boss," Rex said stiffly, "I think this little lady needs changing."

Marissa was grateful for the reprieve. "I'll do it," she said and walked toward the toddler before Grady could respond. Tina outstretched her arms and happily enfolded herself in the embrace. Marissa glanced toward Rex, and the older man's gaze was one of deep concern. It made her feel instantly ashamed. What must Rex think? She wasn't sure why, but his opinion mattered to her. Then Marissa left the stables as swiftly as she could.

Determined to get all thoughts of Grady out of her head. And failed, big-time.

Chapter Six

Grady hadn't expected a lecture from his foreman. But as soon as Marissa had disappeared from sight, he got one, regardless.

"Are you sure you know what you're doin'?"

Grady scowled and closed the stable door. "Your point?"

"She's a nice girl. I don't think she should be messed with."

"Messed with?" Grady stopped midstride and stared at the other man. "You're serious? We're actually gonna have this conversation?"

Rex shrugged. "Needs to be said."

Grady took a deep, irritated breath. "Nothing's going on between me and Marissa," he said quietly. "But if there was, it would be no one's business but ours."

"Didn't look like nothin'," Rex said and slid the saddle off the door. "It looked like somethin'."

"It's nothing," he said again, firmer this time.

But he knew Rex was right. There *was* something going on. Something he had to get control of…and fast.

"Keep the girls occupied, will you?" he asked.

Rex gave a wary nod. "Sure."

By the time he reached the house, Grady's chest had stopped pounding. Until he saw Marissa again. She was in the living room, by the fireplace, staring at the family photographs on the mantel. She looked so effortlessly beautiful in her jeans and ridiculous pink boots. Back in Solo's stall he'd been so close to kissing her. So close to hauling her into his arms and giving in to the desire churning through his blood.

"We need to talk."

Marissa turned slowly and met his gaze. "What about?"

She knew exactly. Grady glanced around the room. "Where's Tina?"

"Down for a nap," she replied and walked to the love seat by the window. She sat down and crossed her legs. "So, talk."

Grady moved across the room and rested his hands on the back of the sofa. "There's something happening here," he said quietly. "Something I don't think either of us expected."

She didn't deny it. In fact, she looked relieved that he'd said the words. But she didn't look happy. Her mouth was compressed into a thin line and her shoulders were tightly bunched.

"Okay—something's happening. It's not worth overthinking it, though," she said after a moment, tossing her hair in that way that got his attention. "It is what it is."

"And what's that?"

She shrugged lightly. "Well...I guess it's sex."

Sex...

So simple. When it felt more complicated than ever. There was color in her cheeks and she was breathing hard. She was trying to stay in control. But Grady wasn't fooled. He knew her. He knew by the way she jutted her chin and held her shoulders tight that she was as caught up as he was. As conflicted as he was. As tormented as he was. "And?"

She shrugged again. "And we've been spending time together this week and at the moment we're both...alone. It's not rocket science, Grady. It's purely a chemical reaction. Just hormones. It's like when Earl got into my yard last week looking for Aunt Violet's cow."

He laughed. "Really? Is that how you see me, Marissa, as some kind of rutting bull?"

She gasped a little. "No, of course not. I only meant that—"

"We're no better than animals in heat?"

"You're twisting my words," she said as she got to her feet and scowled. "I was simply trying to explain—"

"How's this for an explanation," Grady said, cutting her off. "Last night I wanted to kiss you. Twenty minutes ago I wanted to kiss you. And right now," he said as he came around the sofa, "I want to kiss you."

She stepped backward and pressed her legs against the love seat. "But..."

He stopped when he got two feet from her. "But I'm not going to."

"Because of Liz?"

Marissa always demanded the truth of him. Her candor was something he'd always admired. He nodded. "Because it wouldn't be right. It wouldn't *feel* right," he said and placed a hand to his chest. "In here."

It might feel right everywhere else—across his skin and through his blood—but Grady knew that wasn't enough. It would never be enough.

"So, what do we do?" she asked.

"Ignore it. Move past it. Stay away from one another." He shrugged. "Take your pick."

She didn't respond. Didn't as much as blink. But as he

watched her, Grady realized something. She was getting mad. As hellfire. With him. Her brown eyes were suddenly darker than usual and there were splashes of color on her cheeks.

"If you have something to say, Marissa, then say it."

She glared at him and her hands came to her hips. The movement only accentuated her lovely curves, and Grady's gaze moved over her slowly. By the time he met her eyes again she was seething.

She sucked in a breath. "I think… I think you are a manipulative and conceited jerk."

"Because I said I wanted to kiss you? Because I'm honest about being attracted to you?"

Her breath shuddered. "Because you are going to use this *attraction* as a reason to keep me at arm's length and away from the girls."

Irritation rose up his spine. "And why would I do that?"

"Oh, come on, Grady. You've never liked me spending time with them."

"That's not true."

She made a scoffing sound. "Really? Each time I've come back to town in the past two and a half years you've made me feel like I didn't belong with them, like I have no right to be a part of their lives." She flashed him a deathly stare. "Maybe I'm not a relative and there's no blood connection, but I do care about them. I love them. And I promised Liz I'd…"

Her words abruptly trailed off, as if she'd said something she shouldn't have.

Grady stilled. "You promised Liz what?"

She shrugged. "Nothing."

"Don't backpedal," he said, leashing in the resentment coursing across his skin. "What did you promise my wife?"

"It doesn't matter."

Grady stepped closer. "Oh, it matters. What was it?"

She wrapped her arms around her waist and sighed heavily. "I promised her I'd be there for them…to talk to them…to make sure they had—"

"A mommy figure?" he asked, cutting her off.

Grady wasn't quite sure why he was angry. But he was. Marissa's admission felt like criticism. As if he wasn't doing enough for his children. As though he'd failed as a parent. As a father.

"No… Yes… I suppose it was about having someone who could do things with them that a father couldn't…" She sighed heavily as her words trailed off. "You said it yourself," she reminded him. "One day the girls will be older and they will need a woman to talk to about certain things."

She was right. He had said that. But he was still irritated, and the tension between them seemed more amplified than ever.

"I'm sure I'll manage."

"And that puts me in my place, right?" she asked stiffly, shoulders tight. "Fine. Thanks for the lesson today."

Grady felt like kissing her there and then just to stop her from talking. Or leaving.

"Sure. Thanks for taking care of Tina."

He watched her walk out of the room and knew nothing had been resolved. He still wanted to kiss her. Which meant he was still neck-deep in trouble. And didn't see a way out.

"You have to come with us. I insist."

Marissa groaned inwardly. For ten minutes Colleen had been trying to persuade her to join the Parker clan at the town's renaming celebration fair on Friday night. Of course she was tempted to go. There were people in town who she'd once known and being back meant reconnecting with old friends. Plus, it meant time spent with the girls. But it also meant time spent with Grady. And since he was on the top of her "people I must avoid" list, Marissa knew she had to keep her wits and decline the invitation.

Marissa could see Aunt Violet nodding. She'd gone to visit her aunt, and Colleen had arrived minutes later. "I think I'll skip it," she said and smiled at her aunt.

"Nonsense," Colleen admonished gently. "The whole town will be there. It's an important day, and since you're back for good you'll be able to see lots of your old friends..." Her words faded off for a second. "And my granddaughters will be expecting you."

Both the other women were looking at her expectantly. She didn't want to go and make small talk with Grady after the tense way they'd left things. But Colleen's relentlessness eventually wore her down. "Okay. I'll go."

She hadn't seen Grady all week. Which had given her plenty of time to dwell on what had transpired at the ranch. But she missed the girls and looked forward to spending some time with them.

"I'll pick you up," Colleen said. "At three o'clock. That will give us enough time to see the mayor officiate and to find a picnic spot, then eat and settle in for the fireworks. I'm looking after the girls Friday, since Grady is competing in one of the riding competitions."

The renaming celebration was a major event for the town. Twenty years in the making since it was first proposed that the two towns become one, and despite numerous setbacks, the day was drawing close when Cedar Creek and Riverbend would officially be called Cedar River. Marissa knew there was still some resistance among the locals on both sides, but she truly believed that it was what was best for Cedar Creek in the long run. The town needed solidarity, one council, one law office, one name. And with the hospital getting an extension, a new police station being built and another housing development planned, the change would finally help unify the people on both sides of the river.

Friday afternoon she showered, slipped into a long pale blue printed dress and matched it with a pair of tan-colored mid-heeled cowboy boots she'd bought the same time she'd splurged on the hot-pink ones. She wore her hair down and applied some makeup, and when she was done, she stared at her reflection in the bathroom mirror. Stared at the circles under her eyes her makeup failed to camouflage.

She looked tired. Hell, she looked exhausted. *That's what comes from nearly a week of sleepless nights thinking about Grady Parker.*

She loathed thinking it. Hated admitting to herself that he'd been in her dreams more often than not for the past six days. And she didn't know how to get him out.

Marissa shook off the thought and returned to the bedroom, where she packed a small tote, then walked out to the porch to wait for Colleen.

Only, Colleen didn't show.

Marissa watched as Grady's truck pulled up in the driveway and he emerged, looking gorgeous in jeans, a white twill shirt, bolo tie, pale gray Stetson and a belt with a shiny silver buckle. He came through the gate, walked up the path and stopped when he reached the bottom of the steps and saw her on the porch.

"What are you doing here?" she asked warily.

He tilted his hat back and met her gaze. "My mom said you needed a lift." He jacked a thumb in the direction of her Volvo. "She said you had car trouble."

Marissa shook her head. "My car is just fine. Your mother offered to pick me up. She said you were competing today."

"No," he replied cautiously. "I haven't competed for years."

"Then why would Colleen say…" Her words trailed off when his brows came up. Of course. Colleen Parker was matchmaking. "Oh, no. I wish she wouldn't."

"So do I." He shrugged. "But you know my mom. When she gets something in her head…" His words faded for a second. "Well, we should get going."

Marissa shook her head. "It's okay. I'll drive myself, since—"

"I'm here," he said irritably. "So let's go."

I'm here…

He said the words as if his presence was some great prize. Ha! Marissa wanted to toss a shoe at him. "I'd rather not—"

"Not everything has to be an argument, Marissa," he said.

"We agreed that we'd stay away from one another," she reminded him.

"No," he said and propped a foot on the bottom step. "We didn't. It was just one option. And since we are very much a part of each other's life because of my daughters, a stupid option. Unless you plan on staying away from them, too?"

"No, of course I don't." Her skin heated. "But what else can we do? Do you really think we can ignore each other and the…and the…"

"The attraction we have for one another?" He shrugged. "I guess we'll find out as time goes along."

"You think it's that easy?"

"What do you want me to say, Marissa? That I'm going to magically stop thinking that you're beautiful? Or forget about the fact that I want to kiss you?" He blew out a breath. "I'll do my best, okay?"

He sounded as frustrated and as conflicted as she was. But she *wasn't* going to be sympathetic. Or pleased that he'd just said she was beautiful. She wasn't going to *feel* anything. She bit back the rebuttal burning on her tongue, grabbed the small picnic basket she'd left by the door and locked up. It did seem silly, taking two vehicles when they lived so close to one another. Still, neither of them said another word until she was settled in his truck and she realized he'd come alone. "So, where are the girls?"

"My mom picked them up this morning. There was no school today because of the celebrations in town, and I was branding calves this morning."

She nodded and turned her head. "So, you'll talk to your mother?"

Grady started the truck and reversed. "About what?" he asked once they were driving through the gate.

Marissa's jaw tightened. "About her thinking that…that we're…you know…"

"Right for one another?" he supplied. "You try making my mom see sense. She's not listening to me."

It sounded so absurd, Marissa couldn't help laughing softly. "Hasn't she worked out that we'd probably strangle one another if we were…you know…"

He glanced sideways. "I'd never hurt you," he said, more soberly than she expected. "I told you that already."

Guilt snapped at her heels. "I know that. And I didn't mean it in the literal sense. I only meant that…that…most days we don't like each other all that much."

"I thought we'd been through all this. I've never disliked you, Marissa."

Marissa sighed. "Yeah…you like me and you wanted to ask me to prom. I got that."

"You don't believe me?"

She shrugged. "What does it matter now? You took Liz to prom and started dating her, and the rest is history."

"You turned me down. And then you went to prom with Liz's brother, as I recall."

I didn't turn you down...

Liz never told me.

"Kieran O'Sullivan always treated me like a kid sister, and prom was no exception."

"Did you know he was a doctor in Sioux Falls?" Grady remarked.

"Yes," she replied. "We still keep in touch occasionally."

He grunted. "What about the rest of them? Do you still talk?"

Marissa shook her head. "Not much. I saw Liam in town the other day and said hello. Old Man O'Sullivan never really approved of my friendship with Liz. The fact my mom was a mere hairdresser and we lived in a two-bedroom apartment over the salon made me a little lowbrow for the mighty O'Sullivans."

"Liz was never like that, though. In fact, she was the opposite. She had no interest in the money or their position in this town. She and Kieran were the only two worth anything out of the bunch. Liam is as arrogant as the old man and from what I hear Sean is not much better...but at least he's living in LA and not in town."

Marissa nodded. "I used to envy Liz her big family, until I realized how disconnected from them she really felt. From the outside they seemed so normal, but her parents always pushed her to do more, to do better, as though being who she was just wasn't enough. She told me the first time she was genuinely happy was when she married you."

"Did you know the old man almost didn't show up for the wedding?" he said quietly. "Liz had to beg him to give her away at the ceremony. The morning of the wedding Kieran told me he wasn't going to show, so I went to see him at the hotel. Her mom was at the hotel, too, pleading with him, trying to make him see sense."

Marissa's surprise was palpable. "What did you say to him?"

"I told him that I couldn't care less if he showed up or not, but that Liz would be devastated. And that he'd lose her forever."

"He did give her away," Marissa said, remembering her friend's happiness that day. "And she had the wedding she always wanted. She looked so beautiful. You scrubbed up pretty good yourself in that tuxedo."

He laughed. "I don't think I've ever been that worried. I was sure I was going to screw up the vows." He grinned ruefully. "And I did."

Marissa remembered how he'd nervously faltered over some of the words. "You got through it in the end."

He laughed softly. "Hopefully I'll do a better job next time."

"Next time?" Marissa snapped her gaze sideways. "So you *do* want to get married again?"

He shrugged one shoulder. "Maybe. One day."

"I thought you said you didn't want…" Her words trailed. She wasn't sure why her insides were jumping at the idea and quickly pushed the feeling aside. "Your mom will be happy to hear that."

"I said *one day*," he shot back. "Sometime in the future."

"Oh…okay."

She was sure his mouth creased in a smirk. "What about you?" he asked. "You planning on getting married again?"

Thankfully her disastrous relationship with Simon hadn't turned her off the idea altogether. She *did* want to marry again. She wanted a family. Children. A husband. Someone to love. And someone who would love her back with his whole heart.

"Yes. Only…"

"Only?"

She shrugged. "I'll make sure I choose a better sort of man next time."

He was silent for a moment and then spoke. "So, what kind of credentials does he need? Urban or cowboy?"

Heat touched her cheeks. He was teasing…baiting her… seeing how far he could go for some reason of his own. Marissa faked a smile. "Cowboy," she replied. "I was married to a suit and it didn't work out, remember?"

His gaze didn't falter. "Dark or fair-haired?"

She pursed her lips, thinking about her ex-husband's pale blond hair. "Dark."

"Blue or brown eyes?"

"Blue."

"National Geographic or sports channel?"

"Both," she replied. "In moderation."

He grinned fractionally. "Left or right side of the bed?"

Marissa sighed. "No preference. Seeing as I sleep in the middle these days."

He laughed softly. "Me, too. I'm not sure how that happens."

"Maybe because it makes the bed seem less lonely."

He looked at her and she felt the intensity of his stare down deep, through to her bones, her very soul. She wondered how he could do that, or how she allowed it. But the awareness between them had a life of its own. They both knew it. Both felt it. And as much as she was internally battling, Marissa knew that there was no real respite to what she was feeling.

"Well," he said quietly, "I don't imagine you'll be short on guys lining up for a shot."

She tried not to feel insulted. And failed. He had a way of doing that without even trying, she was sure. "What does that mean?"

His mouth twisted. "It means that every cowboy in the

district will be coming out of the woodwork to take their chances with you, Marissa."

"Then you'll have to tell me which ones are worth the effort."

His gaze snapped toward her briefly. "Yeah...right. If you want help finding a husband, ask my mother. She's the one on the matchmaking bandwagon at the moment."

He drove the pickup across the small bridge and headed down Main Street toward the park and fields where the festival was taking place. There were over a hundred vehicles already parked and people milling about, walking toward the main arena where the rodeo was being held. Horse trucks and trailers lined up close by and there was a large stage to the right and a band was playing a George Strait classic. The park to the left was filled with families, many already spread out on blankets or seated at picnic tables.

He parked the truck and they got out. Marissa grabbed the basket and her tote and remembered that she hadn't brought a jacket. The early-autumn breeze was cool. She glanced up at the sky and saw it was clear blue and the afternoon sun shone brightly.

"Where are we meeting your mother?"

He pointed across the parkland. "Under her favorite tree," he replied and grabbed the basket from her. "Let's go."

They walked from the parking area and toward the parkland. She mostly kept up with his long strides, and as they crossed the grass she heard Milly's delighted squeal and they spotted both Milly and Breanna racing toward her, arms outstretched. They reached her in seconds and she hugged the girls close. She knew Grady was watching them, knew he was probably wondering why his daughters were so attached to her. But she knew why—it was Liz. They'd said as much the night she'd gone to the ranch for dinner.

They missed their mother and longed to have that maternal connection with someone. Marissa understood. She'd lost her own mother when she was twelve and had mourned her for a long time. Aunt Violet had tried to fill the void, but Marissa had felt the loss of her parent deeply. Perhaps if she'd had a father she wouldn't have felt so alone. As she looked at the girls skipping beside her, Marissa thought how lucky they were to have such a caring and loving dad. And if Grady got married again, she hoped whoever she was would cherish the three beautiful girls who clearly longed for a mother's love.

She spotted Colleen beside a picnic table and another woman whom she recognized as Brooke, Grady's cousin. Brooke held Tina while Colleen fussed with the food containers on the table. Brant was standing nearby, his left arm still supported by a sling. He was deep in conversation with a couple she recognized as Tanner and Cassie McCord, Grady's neighbors and friends. They had a child with them who looked about a year old and Marissa was sure she spotted a slight baby bump on the other woman. Rex was there, too, standing by the big oak tree, talking with two of the young ranch hands.

Colleen looked up as they approached and smiled. "That was quite a welcome you got."

Marissa smiled back. The girls each held one of her hands and led her around to the side of the table near their grandmother. They made her stand by the table and chatted to her endlessly about their week at school and the impending fireworks. Tina began to cry and she watched as Grady placed the basket on the table and then took the toddler in his arms and gently cajoled her into a delightful giggle. He mopped up the baby's tears when she was done crying and kissed her on the head. And it took two seconds for Marissa's womb to start doing backflips.

Fool.

She pushed the thought aside and concentrated on the girls beside her. After a few minutes they raced around the table to see their father and sister. Colleen poured her a glass of iced tea and patted the seat beside her.

"It's such a shame your aunt couldn't come today," Colleen said quietly and began pulling dishes from the baskets on the table. "She's always been a strong advocate for this merger."

"Are you?" Marissa asked and drank some tea.

Colleen nodded. "I think it will be good for the town… *towns*," she said with emphasis. "When they were both settled in the 1800s, it was the river that kept them apart. Well, there's been a bridge over the river for over one hundred years… It's about time that meant something."

"It means land rezoning," Brooke said and sat opposite.

Colleen nodded. "Yes, there will be changes for some. But I think once—"

"No politics today," Grady said and shifted Tina into his other arm. "Okay, Mom? Brooke? Let's just enjoy the band and the fireworks."

"Easy for some to say," the tall blonde replied, smiling but looking slightly miffed. "You're not losing forty acres of your best grazing land."

Grady shrugged agreeably. "I told you that you can run your herd down the bottom of Flat Rock," he said of the land that ran along the back perimeter of his ranch.

Brooke grinned but still looked defiant. "My land. My herd. My problem."

Grady laughed and ruffled his cousin's hair, and Marissa was warmed by the sense of familial closeness around her. And as Colleen chatted to her and Grady bantered with his cousin while his daughters played nearby, and Brant talked with the McCords, Marissa experienced something she hadn't felt for a long time—*inclusion*. The Parkers were kind, caring people and they welcomed her wholeheartedly.

"My granddaughters are very fond of you," Colleen said softly and continued to pull containers from the baskets on the table.

"I'm very fond of them, too," Marissa said, getting to her feet to help with the task.

"I'm glad. The more people they have who love them, the better."

Marissa glanced toward the girls, saw how they were hanging off their father as he suspended them in the air in turn. "Oh, I think they have plenty of that."

Colleen nodded. "Yes, he's a good father. Better than his own, in fact," Colleen said and then smiled. "Oh, my husband was a lovely man, but he spent too much time working and not enough time with his sons. Grady seems to manage it better, even as a single dad."

Marissa's heart constricted. "Having a father is important."

Colleen's expression softened and she patted her hand. "That was insensitive of me. I'm so sorry. It must have been hard for you to grow up not knowing your father."

She shrugged. "It's gotten easier over time. And I had my mom and Aunt Violet. So I had more than some people ever have."

Colleen smiled. "Janie Ellis was a good person. A little wild at times," she said and winked. "But she used to talk to me when I would go into the salon."

"Did she ever say anything about my dad?"

The other woman nodded slightly. "She never said who he was and I never asked. But once, when she was talking about you, she gave a little sigh and said that despite not knowing him very well, she'd cared for your father. And she loved you more than anything. It was tragic the way she died so young."

Marissa's throat closed over. "Yes. But she knew I'd be safe and well cared for with Aunt Violet. Like you've been there for Grady and the girls since Liz passed away."

"Of course," she replied. "He's my child and I will do whatever I can to see that he's happy." Colleen's eyes sparkled. "Which includes finding him a wife."

Marissa couldn't stop a smile from curving her mouth. "Good luck with that."

Colleen chuckled. "Yes…he's certainly been resistant to the idea so far."

"Maybe not so much," she said and sorted through cutlery. "He told me today he might get married again."

"Really?" Colleen's brows shot up. "He told *you* that?"

She nodded. "He did."

"And would he be married to anyone in particular?" the older woman asked.

Marissa saw her chance to defuse Colleen's matchmaking efforts. "No one in particular."

Colleen's expression feigned innocence for a moment and then the sparkle in her eyes returned. "Well, I shall have to double my efforts."

"Or let him figure it out for himself?" Marissa suggested.

Colleen squeezed her arm. "And let him miss an opportunity? Not a chance."

Marissa had the sinking feeling she was the *opportunity* the other woman was speaking about. "Colleen…this idea you have about Grady and me…it's way off the mark."

She shrugged. "I know what I see. And I know you're probably thinking about Liz and what she would say. But I think she would say it's quite okay."

Marissa wasn't so sure. Liz had kept quiet about Grady wanting to take her to prom in senior year…and even though it happened a long time ago, it was still a cautionary tale. The whole idea was messy and complicated. And after Simon and her bitter divorce, she didn't want complicated. She wanted easy. She'd earned it.

If only she could get Grady out of her head.

Before he gets into my heart.

Too late...

She was shocked by the thought. And distressed. And suddenly terrified. She didn't want to have feelings for Grady. Finding him attractive was hard enough. Anything else was...well...impossible.

"Colleen, I just think it's—"

"My granddaughters need a mom," Colleen said quietly, more seriously. "They need to know what a mother's love means. And with you, they would know that. They love you." She squeezed her hand. "Now all you have to do is get my son to fall in love with you, too."

Marissa gasped. "Oh, that's not—"

"And from the way he's looking at you right this minute," Colleen said, cutting her off, "I don't think that's going to be too hard at all."

Chapter Seven

Grady just knew his mother was up to something. Marissa looked as if she needed rescuing, so he quickly disentangled himself from Breanna and Milly and passed Tina to Brooke. But he was too late—by the time he was around the other side of the table Marissa's face was as red as a beet.

"Feel like checking out the horses before we eat?" he asked and held out his hand.

She looked up, nodded and stood. His mother was grinning, as if she'd gotten exactly what she wanted. *Damn.* He should have known better than to play right into her hands. He loved his mom, but sometimes she drove him to distraction.

Marissa grabbed his hand and he felt her touch right through to his bones. Her hand was small and soft and fit neatly inside his, just as it had over a week ago. There was something so naturally feminine about her, and as she stood and he led her from the table, Grady realized it had a power that threatened to undo him.

Stay away from her.

Ignore her.

Yeah, right. He had more chance of going to the moon than doing that.

"Something you want to tell me?" he asked once they were out of earshot.

She shook her head and pulled her hand from his. "You don't want to know."

He sighed. "I take it my mother was matchmaking again?"

Marissa laughed and the lovely sound carried across the breeze. "Oh, Colleen was doing more than that," she said and kept walking. "She just gave me the green light."

Grady stopped midstride.

The green light?

By the time he started walking again she was ten feet in front of him. He caught up quickly and grabbed her hand. "What does that mean?"

She didn't try to pull away. "The green light…the go-ahead…the stamp of approval."

"I'm sorry, Marissa," he said wearily. "I'll talk to my mom and get her to stop meddling."

Grady met her gaze. Her eyes were bright, as if she was fighting back emotion, and it cut through him with diamond-like precision. He didn't want to see her upset. He had a sudden inexplicable urge to comfort her, and it shocked him to the core. Every past feeling he'd had toward her was shifting, turning, morphing into something else. Something more.

She pulled her hand from his and kept walking. The barrel racing was in full swing, so dust was flying and the sounds of hooves pounding and the audience cheering filled the air. She stood by the bleachers for a moment, arms crossed, eyes cast directly ahead. But he wasn't fooled.

She was no more interested in the horses in that moment than he was.

When he reached her, she took off again, past the bleachers and holding yards and toward the long row of stables. He followed her once more, feeling tension and irritation seep into his blood with every stride.

By the time she stopped she'd walked fifty yards. She pulled up outside an empty stable. Grady reached her and came to a halt. She turned, arms still crossed, eyes still bright.

"Marissa…"

She took a breath and spoke. "Liz never mentioned it."

Grady frowned. "Never mentioned what?"

"About prom," she admitted. "That you wanted to take me."

An uneasy feeling seeped into his gut. The memories were vague but still there. "She told me you weren't interested."

"She lied," Marissa admitted, as if it was the hardest thing she'd ever said.

Grady frowned. "Why would Liz do that?"

"Because she loved you."

It sounded so simple. So innocent. And he had to believe that it was. He'd loved Liz with all his heart. Nothing would change that. But he had to know more. He had to know everything. "And were you?" he asked quietly, moving a little closer. "Interested?"

She stepped back until she was pressed against the stall door. "Sometimes…sometimes for a smart man…you can be a real idiot."

It wasn't an answer. "Yes or no?"

"What does it matter?" she whispered.

"I don't know why it matters," he replied, moving closer. "It just does."

"No," she said quickly, shaking her head. And then softer, raspier, "Yes."

The churning in his stomach increased tenfold. He didn't want to think about what it meant, but his mind wandered... If he had taken Marissa to prom, maybe his life would have played out differently...no Liz, no babies he loved more than life itself. It was impossible to comprehend. Liz did him a favor. Liz always knew what he needed. Liz had been his rock after his father died and when he'd taken over the ranch.

But Liz was gone...

And Marissa was...here. Real. Beautiful. *Tempting*...

Grady stepped toward her and she raised a hand. At first he thought she was pushing him away, but she wasn't. She reached out and rested her palm against his chest, directly over the spot where he knew his heart was beating wildly. And she sighed. A low, heady and wistful sound that reached him deep down, in that place he'd closed off, shut out, ignored for way too long.

And in that moment he couldn't have walked away for anything in the world.

He moved closer, feeling the warmth coming off her skin as he covered her hand with his and held it against his chest. She stared up at him, all shimmering eyes and soft, pink lips. Grady looked at her mouth and saw her bottom lip tremble. He reached for her nape with his other hand and held her steady, stroking the smooth skin at the back of her neck.

And then he kissed her. Softly at first. Almost tentatively. Caution kept him under control. He wanted her permission. He wanted her to tell him it was okay. He wanted her to agree to what was happening between them. And then she did. Her lips parted and she let him inside her sweet, seductive mouth. His tongue found hers and the sensation spiked his libido with such intense force he groaned low in his throat. She felt so good. Tasted so good. And Grady quickly realized something—it didn't feel strange. It didn't feel awkward. Kissing Marissa felt like the most natural and deliciously sensual thing in the world.

He continued to kiss her and kept their mouths connected in the most intimate way, taking and giving, enjoying the soft slide of her tongue against his own, holding her nape gently. The blood in his veins surged, and need overcame everything else. Her hands looped around his neck and he felt her compliance, groaned when her tongue sought his as she pressed closer. He could feel her breasts, her hips, her thighs against him, could feel the heat of her body connecting with his in a way that affected him on some primal level. He wanted her. If he dared to move, he would have walked the three steps into the stall, closed the door and made love to her on the thick bed of hay. But he knew he couldn't. He knew it was going to be only a kiss. And for the moment there was no rush. No reason to stop. Nothing but the two of them, together and wholly connected. When sanity prevailed, he'd release her and pull away. But in those few, intoxicating seconds, Grady was unable to do anything else except keep the connection.

Until he heard Rex's voice behind them.

The guy certainly had a way of showing up at the worst possible time.

"Mrs. Parker is looking for you both."

Grady lifted his head, released Marissa and stepped back. By the time he turned around, Rex was walking away from them. But the older man's tight-shouldered gait spoke louder than words. He didn't approve, not one bit. Perhaps it was some leftover loyalty toward Liz that made Grady feel as if Rex was watching his every move when it came to Marissa. Or maybe he genuinely liked Marissa and was simply looking out for her welfare. Whatever the reason, Grady knew he had to sort it out once and for all.

After he'd figured out what he was going to do about the burning desire he had for the woman in front of him. She was breathing hard and watching him. Glaring, more to the point.

"We should get back," she said flatly. "This is a day for family and celebrations. Not…not…this…not…kissing and craziness…" Her words trailed off and she took a deep breath. "Don't do it again."

"You kissed me back," he said quietly.

She nodded. "So I'm just as guilty. Just as foolish. And right now I'm confused about how I should feel about you. I've programmed myself to think a certain way, *feel* a certain way…and I didn't come back to Cedar River to get caught up in some kind of complicated *thing* with you."

There was pain in her voice—pain and passion and regret. And he was responsible.

She didn't give him a chance to respond and didn't say anything more.

By the time Grady had gotten his thoughts together, she was ahead of him, walking in that straight-backed way that seemed uniquely hers. He caught up as they reached the picnic table where his family were and he knew she was fuming.

He shouldn't have kissed her. Especially out in public where anyone could see. What if one of his daughters had been with Rex? How could he explain it to them? He couldn't. The girls adored Marissa and it would only confuse them. As Marissa was confused. As *he* was confused.

They ate beneath the shade of the big oak while the band played and the music filtered across the parklands. It seemed as if the whole town had turned out for the celebration. Liz had been opposed to the idea of the unification—it was one of the few things they hadn't agreed on. But since the rest of the O'Sullivans were all for the plan, he often wondered if her resistance was simply a knee-jerk reaction to ensure she was at odds with her family. Still, she would have enjoyed seeing the girls so cheerful.

Of course, Grady knew the reason his daughters were happy was because of Marissa. She had their undivided attention. They sat around her at the table, chatting tirelessly, and he admired Marissa's ability to get them to finish their meal without any complaint. She certainly had a way with his children and he knew she'd make a great mom one day.

A great mom...

The words suddenly scrambled around in his head, and as hard as he tried to shake the thought away, it stayed, resolute and clear-cut. Determined. Unyielding. Taunting him. *Tempting him.*

Of course, it was crazy thinking.

It was thinking he needed to forget about...and fast.

Still...the idea lingered. Maybe his mother was right. What if it wasn't such a crazy idea? What if it was the sanest idea he'd ever had? What if it was exactly what he needed, and what she needed, too? Marissa loved his daughters. Marissa was alone. *He* was alone. He was attracted to her. Grady believed it was mutual. And he wanted her in his bed; he wasn't about to deny it. Since she'd come back things had quickly changed between them. They both knew it. And their kiss proved they had an intense physical attraction going on.

Maybe it would be enough to hold them together.

Enough to sustain a relationship.

And enough for a marriage.

I am so not looking at him...

Marissa chanted the words over and over to herself as she interacted with the girls and feigned interest in the food

on her plate. She didn't dare meet his gaze. It was too hard.
Too much. *Too real.*

Grady kissed me.

It was hot. Passionate. Intense.

And I kissed him back.

As if she had a hunger that couldn't be satisfied. As
if she was thirsty and he was water. As if nothing else
mattered for those few, crazy seconds. She wanted him…
more than she'd ever wanted a man before. Not Simon or
the one other boyfriend she'd had before him. Her attraction to Grady was different. Stronger. Deeper. Suddenly
terrifying.

And all she could think was how much she had betrayed
Liz by giving in to the temptation.

It had been building for weeks…and now she'd crossed
the line. Things could never go back to how they once were.
The only thing she could do was stay away, to put distance
between herself and Grady.

Which meant keeping her distance from the girls.

And breaking my promise to Liz.

Which she could never do. The only answer was to stay
strong and not give in to the wayward needs of her libido
when it came to Grady Parker ever again. She'd been strong
before, such as when she'd left her marriage, and she could
be again. She *would* be again.

The mayor officiated the ceremony at five o'clock and
there were speeches from the high school principal and several prominent business owners, including Liam O'Sullivan
and Kayla Rickard, curator of the museum in town and who
was a close friend of Brooke's. Once the speeches were
done, the fireworks started and afterward the rodeo events
resumed. By then the food had been cleared away and the
picnic baskets packed up, and everyone had moved closer
to where the band was playing and the dance floor had been

erected. Colleen took the girls home around seven-thirty and Marissa sat beside Brooke and chatted to the other woman about horses and farming and explained about how her aunt was going to sell the farm and she'd been thinking about taking it on. Grady, Brant and Rex had gone to watch the bull riding, and Marissa was glad for the reprieve.

When the men returned to the table, Brooke convinced Brant to hit the dance floor, although he seemed to go reluctantly. He was a much more serious, brooding version of his older brother, and she was surprised that Brooke got him to agree. The band was playing an upbeat number and Marissa tapped her foot in time with the music.

"Would you like to dance, Miss Ellis?"

Marissa looked to her right. Rex was standing beside the table, one hand extended.

"I'm not much of a dancer," she admitted wryly.

"Me, either," he said and grinned. "Two left feet."

She was embarrassed that he'd caught her making out with Grady but would rather have a dance with him than endure sitting alone at the table with Grady. "Okay."

She looked at Grady. He was on the other side of the table, a drink cradled between his hands, now talking with Tanner and Cassie McCord. But Marissa wasn't fooled. He knew exactly what was going on. She excused herself and took Rex's hand. It was big and rough and calloused and yet remarkably comforting, and as they walked to the dance floor she realized there was something about the older man that made her trust him instinctively.

The tune was upbeat but he took her around the floor in a respectable, almost old-fashioned embrace. She liked that, too. There was nothing improper about Rex Travers.

"You *can* dance," she admonished and grinned.

He shrugged. "A little. My mother taught me when I was young."

"My mother taught me how to braid hair," she said, smiling. "But not how to dance. You're not from around here, though, are you?"

"No," he said and his warm brown eyes darkened a little. "Nevada."

"So, what made you settle in Cedar River?" she asked.

"Seems funny to hear folks calling the place Cedar River," he said and shrugged. "And my reasons for settling here are…kinda complicated."

"Sorry," she said. "I didn't mean to pry."

"Asking questions isn't pryin'," he said, and as he grinned his eyes wrinkled. "Just human nature."

She laughed softly. "That's true. So, how do you like working at the Parker ranch?"

"I like it a lot. He's a good boss. Miss Liz was nice, too…a real kind sort of person. I miss havin' her around the ranch. Boss misses her, too."

"She was my closest friend," Marissa said quietly. "And I know Grady misses her."

Rex nodded. "And sometimes missing someone can make a man do things he wouldn't normally do."

Marissa nodded, immediately understanding the caution in his words. Rex cared about Grady and Liz's memory, and as much as she tried to be annoyed at his interference, she simply couldn't. "I know you probably want to protect Liz, but I promise you I—"

"It ain't Miss Liz I'm trying to protect," he said, cutting her off. "It's you."

"I don't understand…" Marissa's words trailed and she met his gaze.

And in that moment she felt a pull, a connection so intense it made her numb all over and she stopped moving. His brown eyes, suddenly sad and earnest, gazed deeply into hers. She couldn't fathom the feelings running riot across her skin and through her blood. And suddenly she had the urge to run. To get away. Before he said anything else. Before she heard anything else. Her breath caught in her throat and suddenly she couldn't get enough air into her lungs.

What is happening?

She dropped her hands and shook her head. "I…I can't… I have to go."

Then she turned and fled, as fast as she could without making a scene.

By the time Marissa made it to Grady's truck, she was breathing so hard she thought her heart might burst through her chest. She slumped against the passenger door and drew in long gulps of air.

It made no sense. There was nothing threatening about Rex. But still, for those few seconds she'd felt threatened. Oh, not physically…but by something else…something she couldn't fathom. Something she didn't dare to think about.

"Marissa?"

Grady's voice startled her and she jumped. "Oh…hi."

He was frowning. "What's wrong? You took off like a frightened rabbit. What happened? Did Rex say something to upset you? Did he do something that—"

"No," she said quickly. "He didn't do anything."

Grady's expression was unchanged. "But he *said* something?"

"I'm not sure," she said slowly.

"What does that mean?"

"It means, I'm not sure," she said again. "I don't know what happened. We were dancing, and then we were talking about Liz, and I—"

"Liz?" he echoed. "Why the hell were you talking about Liz?"

"We were talking about you and the ranch and then…

I don't know…it just got *weird*. I can't explain it." She met his gaze. "But please, don't say anything to him about it."

He shook his head. "What would I say? You haven't told me anything."

She relaxed a little. "It's nothing, I promise. I would like to go home now, if that's okay?"

He didn't look entirely convinced, but he nodded. "Sure. I have your bags," he said and passed her the tote and small basket.

By the time she got into the truck and buckled up the seat belt, her breathing had returned to normal. They drove back in silence, and once he'd pulled up outside her house he jumped out and quickly came around the passenger side. Marissa grabbed her things and walked ahead.

As the porch sensor light came on, she pulled the keys from her tote, climbed the steps and opened the door. She had no plans to invite him inside. Temptation would be left on the doorstep.

"Thanks for the lift."

"Marissa? We should talk about—"

"I don't want to talk," she said wearily. "It's been a long afternoon and I want to go to bed." She stopped, stilled and met his gaze head-on. "Alone."

His eyes darkened. "You sure about that?"

She wasn't sure about anything. And for a second she *was* tempted to invite him inside and do what she knew they both wanted.

"Positive."

He didn't budge. "I think we both know it's inevitable, right?"

"What's inevitable?"

"That at some point we're going to make love."

Marissa longed for the ground to open up and swallow her. He said it so casually, so matter-of-factly, when she was dying inside. He clearly had no regard for her feelings. "Nothing is inevitable. That would mean we had no control over it…and we do. *I do.* I won't betray my best friend."

His gaze narrowed. "You think you'd be betraying Liz by making love with me?"

"Of course I would. *We* would."

He shook his head so slowly it was excruciating. "This hasn't got anything to do with Liz."

"Of course it does."

He moved closer. "No…it doesn't. Liz is gone. And this is about you and me."

Marissa stepped back. If he touched her, she'd crumble. "And that's a convenient line to use when you're trying to get laid."

"It's not a line," he said quietly. "It's the truth. And I'm not trying to get laid, Marissa. There's more between us than that. Or at least there could be, if you'd let yourself off the hook and stop feeling guilty."

There's more between us than that.

It sounded perfectly reasonable. It sounded like exactly the words she wanted to hear. But they were *only* words. He wanted to get her into bed. That was all he wanted. And Marissa wanted more. She wanted… She wanted everything. And she knew, deep in her heart, that she'd never get it.

Because Grady would never love her. He might *want.* He might even *need.* But Liz had his heart and always would.

"There's nothing between us," she said and closed the door without looking back.

Grady had been back at the ranch for precisely two minutes when he went looking for Rex. He knew the other man was back, because his old pickup was parked by the side of the stables. Grady strode around and tapped on the door of the biggest of the three small houses he'd had built for the ranch hands ten years earlier. As foreman, Rex got his own place.

He needed to know what had happened with Marissa. First, because he was so wound up he could barely stand being in his own skin. And second, because he cared about Marissa and didn't like knowing she was upset.

I care about Marissa...

That's what was messing with his head. The attraction he could handle. Sex was easy to compartmentalize. But caring...that was different. That was the kind of thing that made a man say and do stupid things. Reckless things. Such as making promises. And wanting commitment because being around her felt *right*. Seeing the way she was with his girls did something to him deep inside. And it would be easy to imagine being with her given how much he desired her.

Except she didn't feel the same way.

There's nothing between us.

He didn't need to hear *that* again to get the picture.

The door opened before he could dwell any more on how cold and controlled she had sounded. Grady crossed the threshold without an invitation. "We need to talk."

Rex didn't say a word until they were down the narrow hall and in the kitchen. "Sure, boss. What about?"

Grady turned on his heels. "You tell me," he shot back. "You tell me why Marissa ran off from the dance tonight."

Rex shrugged. "I'm not sure."

"Yeah, that's what she said." Grady's blood heated. He liked Rex, but he wanted answers. And fast. "But I didn't believe her, either."

Rex sat down at the small table. "I don't know why. We were talking and then she left."

Grady rested against the small counter. "She was upset when I found her."

The older man looked genuinely concerned. "She was cryin'?"

"No," Grady replied, irritation rising through his system. "But she was clearly upset. Why? What did you say to her?"

Rex linked his rough hands and set them on the table. "We were talkin' about—"

"Liz," Grady said, cutting him off. "Yeah, I got that from Marissa. What I don't get is why."

Rex shrugged. "I didn't mean to upset her."

Grady crossed his arms, pushed down the annoyance rising in his blood and spoke. "I'd like to know why you think it's okay to discuss my wife with Marissa."

"Ain't no malice intended," Rex said quietly. "We were just talkin'."

Grady didn't believe him. "You've been working here for over six years and in that time you haven't struck me as a man who likes to do a whole lot of talking. So why now?" he asked. "And why with Marissa?"

Rex got to his feet, let out a long sigh and dropped his shoulders. "I've got my reasons."

He pushed himself off the counter. "I'm sure you have. I'd just like to know what they are. I don't want to see Marissa get hurt."

Rex scowled. "From what I've seen, it ain't me that's gonna hurt that girl."

Grady stilled, took a breath and ignored the anger in his belly. "What does that mean?"

"You know exactly," Rex replied, harder than usual. "You're messin' with her feelings. I ain't too smart about some things, but I can see she's confused and scared, and after everythin' she's been through, it seems to me that you should back off and leave her be."

Everything she's been through?

Had Marissa confided in Rex about her marriage? It

didn't seem likely. As far as he knew they were only barely acquainted, and Grady's confusion quickly turned into concern. Alarm bells rang in his head. Had Rex been spying on Marissa? Was he infatuated with her? Hell, he didn't really know anything about the older man other than he was a good horseman and seemed like a straight shooter. But maybe he'd been wrong. His anger gathered momentum and turned into a hot, unrelenting rage. This man had been in his home…had interacted with his children. Had he trusted someone he shouldn't have?

"What do you know about it?" he demanded, stepping closer.

Rex shrugged. "Enough."

"But how do you know?" Grady asked, clenching his fists. "Tell me, damn it!"

Rex stepped back and pressed a palm to his chest. His brown eyes were glazed. "Because I feel it…in here."

Grady wondered if the other man was going to break down. He looked breached, broken. And Grady was sure he saw tears in his eyes. "What the hell are you talking about, Rex? This doesn't make sense. You hardly know Marissa. Why are you suddenly acting like her white knight?"

Rex met his gaze. "I ain't her white knight," he said quietly. "I'm her father."

Chapter Eight

Grady stared at the other man. What the hell was Rex talking about? Marissa didn't have a father.

But there was no dishonesty in Rex's expression.

Only truth.

And sorrow.

Grady swallowed hard. "Are you sure?"

Rex nodded. "Positive. But you can't tell her. She doesn't know, and when she hears it, she has to hear it from me."

He agreed. If it were true, Grady knew Marissa would be shocked. And hurt. The very idea made him ache inside.

"When are you going to tell her?" Grady demanded.

"Soon," Rex assured him. "When the time feels right."

"How about right now?" he suggested.

Rex shook his head. "She needs to know she can trust me before I tell her who I am."

"And how are you going to do that?" he asked. "By hanging around her farm doing yard work and asking her to dance every chance you get?"

Rex's brown eyes darkened. "I'm not going to hurt her with this news if I can help it. But I will tell her...and soon."

Grady wanted to believe it. "Is that why you came to Cedar River six years ago?"

"I was passin' through," Rex admitted. "I was at the Loose Moose having a beer and bumped into a couple of old ranch hands I used to know. We got to talkin' and I found out that Janie Ellis had a daughter twenty-five years earlier and worked it out from there. So I got this job and stayed in town."

"Without telling anyone?"

Rex nodded. "Not a soul. Only Violet Ellis knows the truth, and she ain't about to say anything."

Miss Violet knew? Grady's insides churned. The whole thing was getting more complicated with every passing second.

Marissa deserved to be told the truth, but Grady felt it wasn't his place to say anything. Rex had always seemed to be a decent and honorable man, and he clearly didn't want to hurt Marissa. So, he'd wait for Rex to do the right thing and ensure he was there to handle the fallout. Marissa would need him, no doubt about it. And he'd be there for her even if she didn't want him to be.

Marissa spent Saturday packing boxes and cleaning out the two spare rooms in the house. Sunday morning she spent with her aunt, going over her plans to move into the retirement villa within the next few weeks. It was all organized and she was happy for Violet. She still had to make a decision about the ranch and there were plenty of reasons why it was a good idea. She needed a home and the farm had been a home for her when she was a child. And whatever she decided, Marissa was looking forward to the next phase in her life.

New beginnings.

Exactly what she needed.

But she couldn't quell the unease in her heart—although she didn't say anything to her aunt. And on the way home from the hospital, she stopped to visit Liz.

The cemetery was just on the outskirts of town, only a short detour. There were a number of cars in the parking area, and once she'd parked Marissa grabbed her tote and walked through the stone gates. Liz was laid to rest near the rest of the O'Sullivans. It was one concession that Grady had made to her grieving parents, and she knew it had been a difficult decision for him.

Marissa stood by the ornate white marble headstone. *Elizabeth Ann O'Sullivan Parker. Daughter, wife, mother. Much loved and forever in our hearts.* There were several fresh flowers resting against the headstone and she wondered if Liz's parents had been by that morning.

Marissa closed her eyes and said a prayer for her dearest friend. Her own mother was buried on the other side of the hill in much less grand circumstances. As were the grandparents she'd never met. But it was always Liz she came to see. Liz, who had been there like no one else when her mother had died. Who understood how much she'd longed for a proper family.

What would her friend think if she knew her thoughts? Her dreams?

Her desires...

Marissa had so many thoughts running through her mind and heart. About herself. About her new life. About Grady. Wanting him was one thing, but the realization that it was more than that...well, it was hard to keep the idea from invading her thoughts 24/7. She hadn't expected to have feelings for him. But she did.

I'm falling in love with him...

Admitting it was both cathartic and terrifying.

"Marissa?"

A deep voice jerked her from her thoughts. *Grady.* She pivoted on her heels. He was standing about six feet away. He was dressed in dark jeans, a blue shirt and a jacket. He looked familiar and attractive, and she experienced the usual fluttering in her belly.

"Are you okay?" he asked.

She nodded. "Fine. I just came to pay my respects. But I don't want to intrude, so—"

"You're not intruding," he said, cutting her off. "I came by earlier. I've been down at my dad's grave with my mom and Brant."

Marissa stepped back and smiled fractionally. "Are the girls with you?"

"With my mother and Brant," he replied. "They spent a few hours this morning with Liz's folks, but I bring them to see their mom every month. It's for Breanna mostly… She remembers Liz and seems to get comfort from coming here. While she's still asking to come and see her mother, I'll bring her. They like to bring daisies."

Marissa's heart contracted and she looked at the three small posies again. "They were Liz's favorite."

"Yes. Even though she was never one for flowers and gifts, she did love daisies."

Marissa fondly remembered how her down-to-earth friend had often looked dismayed at the frivolous gifts Marissa always brought back from New York when she visited. But Marissa had playfully ignored Liz's protests that she was spoiling them all with her generosity. "Liz would love that you bring them here. You're a good dad, Grady. Better than you realize, I think."

His blue eyes darkened. "Thank you. But you know,

being their dad is the greatest gift I've ever received. Being a parent is very humbling."

"I'm sure it is."

"One day you'll discover for yourself," he said and moved closer. "When you have a baby of your own."

The idea had her womb rolling over. "Maybe...one day."

She stepped onto the path, said a final goodbye to Liz and walked away. Grady walked in step, and the silence between them was suddenly deafening. She didn't want to talk to Grady about having babies. Because suddenly the only babies she wanted to have were his!

"So," she said, shifting the subject, "why are you all dressed up?"

"I've been a contract brand inspector for a few years," he explained as they walked. "I had a meeting in town earlier."

"You mean cattle brands?" she queried.

"Exactly. Mitch Culhane and I do most of the inspecting in this county."

Marissa knew the Culhanes owned a ranch even bigger than Grady's on the other side of town and she'd gone to school with a few of the Culhane brothers. "Working on a Sunday?" she teased. "That's commitment."

He shrugged in that loose-limbed way of his. "Just another day. And I was coming into town anyway, to drop my kids at my in-laws."

By the time they reached the gates, the girls had already spotted her and came running. Breanna and Milly hugged her close just as Colleen was putting Tina into the backseat of her car.

"It's lovely to see you, Marissa. We're having lunch together at my place," Colleen said, smiling. "Would you like to join us?"

Marissa felt faintly embarrassed by the idea of being included so impromptu. She looked at Grady, but he was ten feet away having a conversation with his brother. "Oh, I wouldn't want to intrude on—"

"Nonsense," Colleen said gently. "You could never intrude. And the girls would love to spend some time with you."

Breanna and Milly chorused their grandmother's words, and before she had a chance to decline they all had climbed into their vehicles and were driving off. Marissa lingered in the parking lot for a minute or so before she started the Volvo and headed into town. When she arrived at Colleen's, the girls were waiting by the front steps and Grady was sitting on the love seat on the porch, with Tina in his arms.

His gaze followed her up the path and she was excruciatingly aware of his scrutiny. She stopped at the bottom of the steps and got another hug from the girls before their father told them to go inside.

When they were out of sight, she spoke. "Sorry to crash your party."

His gaze was unfaltering and he rocked in the love seat while the toddler dozed against his chest. "You know very well everyone wants you here."

She shrugged a little. "Well, Breanna, Milly and your mom."

"Everyone," he said again.

Heat smacked her cheeks and she held her breath. He had a way of making everything sound sexy. A way of making her forget every reason why she shouldn't be attracted to him.

Why she shouldn't fall in love with him.

She pulled herself together. "I'll go and see if your mom needs any help."

He didn't move. "I'm sure she'd like that."

Marissa took off as if her feet were on fire. She didn't want to be constantly uncomfortable around Grady, but their relationship was heading that way. She didn't make it to the kitchen, though—the girls waylaid her in the hall-way and dragged her into one of the bedrooms that had been converted into a playroom. It had everything a little girl could want—a dollhouse, a sketching easel, a wardrobe filled with dress-up clothes, and a small table and chairs for tea parties. Marissa couldn't help smiling. The huge dollhouse looked as though it had been handcrafted and she was pretty sure Grady had made it for his daughters.

She sat on the narrow bed and allowed Breanna to place a tiara on her head and for half an hour laughed and clapped as the girls dressed up and danced and twirled and had a marvelous time. Marissa painted Milly's nails and watched as Breanna rummaged through the wardrobe for what she said was the perfect princess outfit.

It was, in fact, a wedding dress. Vintage style, with a lace bodice and long chiffon train that fell from the hips. Colleen's old dress, she suspected, which Breanna quickly confirmed.

"Nan lets us wear it anytime," Breanna said and frowned a little. "It's too big, though." The little girl's eyes widened. "But not for you. Put it on. Put it on," she chanted quickly.

"Yes," Milly insisted and started jumping up and down as she usually did. Marissa had little chance of refusing as both girls started twirling around the room, laughing and pleading. She slipped the gown over her own dress and was surprised that it actually fit quite well. Breanna zipped her up and Milly placed a pair of satin shoes by her feet. She ditched her sandals and put them on—they were a little tight, but the girls were having such a delightful time she didn't have the heart to complain.

Breanna handed her a long lace veil, and once she'd placed it on her head Marissa checked herself in the mir-ror by the bed. Even though the gown was lumpy in parts because of her other dress underneath and the shoes were tight and the veil had a couple of tears in it, she still couldn't help smiling at her reflection. There was something utterly romantic about a wedding gown—even if it was simply make-believe.

"Wow," Breanna said, her expression filled with pure joy. "You really do look like a princess."

"Actually," a deep voice said from the doorway, "you look like a bride."

Marissa turned and almost toppled off the heels. Grady stood in the doorway, arms crossed, one shoulder resting against the architrave. He was regarding her with such burning intensity she couldn't have looked away even if she'd wanted to.

"Ah…where's Tina?" she asked, conscious of the heat in her cheeks and the trembling in her knees.

"Right here," he said as the toddler peeked out from behind his legs and raced into the room. "But since she's been a little cranky this morning she's going to go down for a real nap once she's had lunch." His mouth turned up at the edges. "Are you having fun?"

She nodded. "Absolutely."

Breanna rushed toward her father and tugged at his elbow. "Daddy, doesn't Marissa look like a beautiful princess?"

"She does indeed," he said, his gaze unmoving. "Very beautiful."

Marissa managed a smile. But the tension between them was palpable and she knew he felt it as much as she did. "Apparently it's your mother's dress."

"It is," he said, still not moving, still watching. "The girls love this room. Grown-up girls, too, by the look of things."

She laughed softly. "The idea of being a princess for ten minutes was way too tempting."

"What about being a bride?" he asked, his voice so low she was sure he meant the words for her alone. "Is that tempting, too?"

Yes.

But she didn't say it. Because she wouldn't have been able to reply and hide the longing in her voice. He could never know. Not ever.

"I should get out of this costume and go help your mom," she said instead.

Before she had a chance to ask Breanna to unzip the gown, Grady had instructed his eldest daughter to take her younger sisters to the kitchen. Once the children had left the room, he pushed himself off the doorjamb and moved behind her.

"Need some help?" he asked quietly.

Marissa was about to respond when she felt his knuckles against her back as he slowly unzipped the dress. Of course it should have been perfunctory and harmless. But it didn't feel like either of those things. It felt…seductive. It felt…good. And in that moment she could easily imagine Grady stripping off the rest of her clothes and then falling into bed with him.

The gown dropped to her feet and she quickly stepped out of it and smoothed down her own dress that had been underneath. Then she scooped up the gown and placed it on the narrow bed. "Thanks," she said and sat on the bed so she could take off the shoes.

Grady was beside the bed in a second, crouched at her knees wordlessly, her left foot in his hands. "You know," he said, so softly she bent closer to hear the words, "you look incredibly pretty in a tiara."

Marissa realized she still had the tiara and veil on her head and her fingers immediately came to her temple. "Breanna insisted," she said.

"My daughter wants what she wants," he said and slowly removed her shoe. "She's a lot like her father in that way."

Marissa's breath caught in her throat. "And what is it that you want?"

His gaze was unfaltering. "Oh, Marissa," he said as he removed the other shoe. "I think you know."

There was so much sexual promise in his voice that she shuddered. He held her foot and ran a thumb slowly along the arch, and his touch made her moan. "Please…" The word was barely audible. "Stop."

Grady released her immediately and stood. "Okay. But when you're ready, Marissa…just let me know."

She looked up and pulled off the tiara and veil. "Ready? For what?"

"For this," he replied and waved a hand. "For us."

Us?

It sounded so real. So…normal. But it was a dream. A fantasy. "We…can't."

He shrugged loosely. "Why not?"

"Because," she said and got to her feet. "It wouldn't be right."

"For who?" he asked. "You? Me? The girls? My mom?" He turned and ran a clearly frustrated hand through his hair. "Damn it, Marissa, half my family is already in love with you."

But not you.

Because Grady's heart belonged to someone else. And always would.

"What do you think, Grady?" she shot back. "That just because your kids and mother like me that's enough reason for us to jump into bed together. Well," she said, hands on hips, "it's not."

"I'm not talking about *jumping into bed together.*"

She stilled. "Then what?"

He shrugged loosely. "Honestly…I don't really know… All I know is that seeing how happy my daughters are when they are around you has made me realize I'd be foolish to ignore what's been happening between us these past couple of weeks."

Her insides were jumping, her hands were shaking and her heart was aching. And she had no idea what he meant. If it wasn't about sex, if it wasn't about the attraction that seemed to have suddenly developed a will of its own, then what was it?

She took a deep breath. "Do you want to date me because your children would approve? Is that it?"

"I think so…yes."

I think so.

Such commitment!

Marissa glared at him. He truly did have an ego as big as South Dakota. "Tempting offer, but no, thanks."

He actually looked surprised. "No?"

She stood her ground. "No."

"One date…it's just a place to start," he said, brows raised. "Don't you think?"

"I'm not about to start anything with you. And I'm going to forget we've had this conversation," Marissa said as she shook her head, got some gumption in her back and headed for the door. But he called her name and she stopped before she crossed the threshold. "What?"

"I meant what I said," he replied. "Only when you're ready for this, and not before."

Marissa gave him a death stare. "You have some ego, you know that? And why this sudden change? Two weeks ago you said you weren't interested in anyone."

"I don't think I said that exactly. You asked if I still felt married to Liz," he reminded her. "And I said people simply didn't turn off feelings."

"I know what you said, Grady," she shot back. "But why now? And why me?"

He stared at her, deeply, intently, as if there was nothing else and no one else. "Because I think you're beautiful. Because my daughters adore you. Because I want you in my bed."

And she knew, right then, that he thought that would be enough. But if she said that, if she admitted that she wanted more...that she wanted everything...then he would guess the truth. And Grady knowing she was falling in love with him would be too humiliating to bear.

"It wouldn't be right," she said again. "Liz would—"

"Liz is gone," he said, cutting her off. "And neither of us can hide behind her now."

"I'm not hiding."

"Sure you are," he said quietly. "And for far too long I've done the same. But..."

"But what?" she asked hotly. "Now you've had some big awakening and want someone to warm your bed?"

"Not someone," he replied quietly. "You."

She laughed humorlessly. "That's ludicrous."

"You can deny it, but the truth is that there's something between us...something I'm not prepared to ignore any longer."

She didn't want to hear it. It was too rational. Too much. "Like I said, I'm going to forget we've had this conversation." She flipped the words out and then left the room. Legs shaking. Heart breaking.

Grady had no luck finding a new housekeeper. He'd interviewed three people in the past two weeks and none were suitable. Two wanted a room-and-board situation, which he wasn't offering, and the other made it clear she wasn't keen on younger children. On Wednesday afternoon he called the employment agency in Rapid City and asked them to find a few more candidates. And until he found someone he'd continue to work around the girls' school schedule the best he could, with a little help from his mother, his brother and the McCords. And Marissa.

Just thinking about her set his blood on fire.

Three days after his disastrous attempt to ask her out, Grady was still thinking about how beautiful she'd looked in the girls' playroom, dressed in his mom's old wedding gown. There'd been a vulnerability in her eyes and he wanted only to comfort her. Instead, he'd made some vague pass and glossed over what he really meant to say.

Mostly because he didn't know what the hell to do with what he was feeling.

And since he now knew the truth about Rex, it added a whole new level of complication to the situation. He felt she needed to be told, but Rex insisted it wasn't the right time. Only, Grady wasn't so sure. Marissa wanted a family and Rex was her father. But it still wasn't his place to tell her…despite how much he was compelled to let her know the truth.

He'd given her space for a few days, but he had Breanna's school play on Thursday afternoon, and since his mother was on the drama committee for the school, Grady called Marissa and asked if she'd look after Tina for a few hours. She agreed without hesitation and he dropped his daughter off just after two o'clock.

She came to the door in long denim shorts and a bright red T-shirt that molded her curves like a second skin. She had bright red loafers on her feet and her hair was caught up in a ponytail. She looked vibrant and healthy and too sexy for words.

"Thanks for doing this," he said and walked into the house with a sleeping Tina in his arms. "I didn't want to take her to the school as she's been a bit cranky this morning and has been dozing off and on for the past hour or so."

Marissa nodded and ushered him into one of the small bedrooms, and he gently placed his daughter on the bed while Marissa shifted pillows around her. He dropped the bag with Tina's things by the door.

"She'll probably sleep for another hour or so," he said and passed Marissa a small food carrier. "Her favorite snacks and drinks and her toys are in the bag."

"Okay...no problem."

Grady lingered by the door. "Any problems, send me a text and I'll call you back."

He leaned forward and kissed her cheek. It should have just been a friendly peck, but when it came to Marissa, his feelings had gone way beyond friendship. But she didn't flinch. Didn't react.

Tempting offer...but no, thanks...

Her words from a few days earlier were now indelibly imprinted in his brain.

No, thanks...

Right. She's not interested. And she'd accused him of being egotistical, which he'd never considered himself to be. A healthy ego, maybe. But he could have sworn she was as wrapped up in the attraction between them as he was. Maybe not.

He left without another word and spent the next few hours helping set up the staging in the school gym for the play, and then the following hour watching his eldest daughter perform the role of a dancing sunflower in a costume his mother had fashioned. Milly sat with him and he'd even dragged Brant from his usual hibernation to spend some time with the family. It was intermission before he had a chance to check his phone and saw three messages from Marissa.

He left Milly with his brother and headed outside the gymnasium. He spent precisely twenty seconds on the phone with Marissa before he ended the call and headed inside to find his brother.

"I have to bail," he said when he found Brant. "Can you make sure Milly and Breanna get to Mom's tonight?"

Brant nodded and frowned. "Sure...what's wrong?"

"Tina's sick. I gotta run."

Fifteen minutes later Grady was back at Marissa's, wondering how he hadn't gotten a speeding ticket along the way. Marissa met him at the front door, looking pale and worried.

"She has a fever," she said as he strode through the doorway. "I tried cooling her down in a tepid bath, but I don't think it helped."

Grady was by his daughter's side in seconds. She moaned and called him Daddy, and his heart just about broke in two. He pressed his hand to her forehead. She did have a fever and her cheeks were hot and pink. The swiftness of the fever concerned him and he quickly bundled her up in a soft cotton blanket.

"I think I'll just take her straight to the ER," he said and stood. "The fever came on quickly, so better to be over-cautious."

Marissa nodded. "I'll come with you," she said and followed him down the hallway.

Once they were at his dual cab truck, Marissa ducked into the backseat. "I'll sit with her," she said and held out her arms. "You drive."

On the way to the hospital she held his daughter as if she was the most precious thing in the world, and seeing the love she had for his child turned him inside out. No one, he realized, no woman he might ever become involved with, would ever love his children with the depth that Marissa did. By the time they reached the small community hospital, it was after eight o'clock. Grady parked illegally in the loading bay but didn't care, and he quickly carried his daughter into the emergency room while Marissa kept pace at his side.

He was relieved to see Dr. Monero on duty. He'd known Lucy since they were kids and trusted her. Years ago her parents had owned a neighboring ranch, which had been sold off when her father died and Lucy and her mom moved into town. Tina, he was sure, was in the best of hands. It was barely minutes before Tina was laid out on a bed in triage to be examined. Grady was allowed to stay by her side, and he held his daughter's hand as tests and consultations with other doctors were done. She cried and moaned and he experienced such an acute sense of helplessness it was almost excruciating to breathe. Marissa remained close by, and he was grateful for her silent support.

But when Tina's fever spiked again and she convulsed, he was quickly ushered out of the cubicle while a medical team attended to her. It was the longest five minutes of his life. And Marissa, quiet and stoic at his side, grabbed his hand and squeezed his fingers as they waited.

When Dr. Monero came out to see him, she looked calm but concerned.

"Tina suffered a febrile convulsion," she explained, and he heard Marissa gasp as she squeezed his fingers tighter. "It often happens when an infant has such a high temperature. A fever occurs when the body is trying to fight infection. This appears viral rather than bacterial, but we've done a few swabs just to be sure."

Viral. Bacterial. Swabs. Grady's head felt as if it was going to explode.

"Is she going to be okay?"

Lucy Monero nodded. "I think so. The convulsion is

kind of like a coping mechanism against the fever. We'll monitor her here for the next six hours, and if I'm not happy with her response to treatment we'll look at moving her to the hospital in Rapid City," she said, calm and matter-of-fact. "Their pediatric department has a number of specialists and is better equipped than ours. But for the moment we'll wait and see."

"Can I see her now?"

"Of course."

Grady spent the following five hours by his daughter's bedside, sitting in an uncomfortable chair, not speaking. Marissa sat at his side. Together. Hands linked and sharing the distress of seeing his child so ill and vulnerable. Medical staff worked around them, not saying much, but offering concerned and sympathetic looks.

Dr. Monero returned after midnight and informed them that they had decided to transport Tina to the bigger hospital in Rapid City.

"It's more precautionary than anything else," she explained. "Her temperature is still high and if she convulses again I think having a pediatric specialist on hand will be an advantage." She patted Grady's arm reassuringly. "But I'm sure she's going to be fine."

Grady trusted Lucy's judgment and agreed with her decision. While they prepared Tina for the journey in the ambulance, he stood back—and Marissa remained at his side. His hand was numb from holding hers, but he didn't release the grip. It soothed him. Calmed him. Her presence made an unbearable situation almost endurable.

"I'll drive your truck," Marissa said quietly. "You travel in the ambulance with her."

He nodded and twenty minutes later they were on their way to Rapid City. When they arrived at the hospital, he called his mother, knowing she would still be awake and worried, even though it was nearly two in the morning. He felt better once he knew Breanna and Milly were okay and reassured Colleen that Tina would be fine.

Marissa met him in the children's ward and they were quickly shown to Tina's room. She lay asleep, her tiny chest rising with every breath. Grady stalled in the doorway, his lungs so tight and his throat so choked with emotion he could barely breathe. Marissa must have sensed his apprehension, because she placed a hand on his shoulder and urged him forward.

Walking toward his sick child…those were some of the hardest steps he'd ever taken. The whole situation reminded him too much of the last precious hours he'd spent with Liz…of Breanna's despair and Milly's confusion…of his mother-in-law crying in the hall…of the pain in his heart.

He pushed the memory away and sat in the chair by the bed, while Marissa took a seat on the other side. The room seemed eerily quiet. The echoes of footsteps over the floor outside the room and the methodical beep of a monitor next door were all he could hear. That and his child's breathing… haunting him, amplifying his helplessness.

Half an hour passed. A doctor came and went. A nurse returned every ten minutes to place cool compresses on Tina's skin. Once the nurse left the room, Marissa stood and moved to the window. It was still dark outside—dawn was a couple of hours away. Grady was tired but knew he'd never sleep—not until he was sure his baby was out of danger.

He got up, stretched his legs and went to join Marissa. She had her back to him, arms crossed, staring out into the street below.

"Are you okay?" he asked.

She nodded, stilled and then shook her head. "I feel so responsible."

Grady's chest ached and he placed his hands on her shoulders. "Why? This isn't your fault."

She turned and he saw tears in her eyes. "Tina was in my care. I was supposed to be watching over her."

Grady took a deep breath, grasped her chin and raised her gaze to his. "Marissa, you did everything right. You tried to cool her down as soon as you realized she had a fever. You called me straight away. You did nothing wrong," he assured her. "Okay?"

Her lower lip wobbled. "But I—"

"Nothing," he said, and then before he could talk himself out of it, he kissed her softly.

It was comfort and sweetness. It was about finding solace for a few brief moments. Her lips moved over his, tentative, but searching, seeking. Something stirred within him, the knowledge they were two people drawn together, needing one another, needing closeness.

Grady finally pulled back gently and held her against him.

"I'm so glad you're here," he said softly.

She sighed against his chest. "I wouldn't be anywhere else."

Her words gave him inexplicable comfort. Peace. And something else.

Hope.

Chapter Nine

When Marissa woke up, her neck was stiff and her arms were numb. The narrow hospital chair wasn't designed for sleeping. She sat up and stretched and then got to her feet. Grady was in the chair opposite, eyes open, watching her.

She looked at Tina, still asleep. "How is she?" Marissa asked and stepped close to the bed.

"Better," he said and stood. "Her fever dropped this morning around eight o'clock."

Relief coursed through her and she managed a smile as she gently touched Tina's forehead and felt it cool against her palm. "What time is it now?"

"Ten."

Marissa met his gaze, saw his weary expression and frowned. "Did you get any sleep at all?"

He glanced at the chair by the bed. "Not really. I couldn't sleep until I knew she was out of danger. And since then…" His words trailed off and he sighed heavily. "I've just been looking at her and thanking God that she's okay."

The baby stirred and opened her eyes. "Daddy."

He stepped closer to the bed and cupped Tina's head with his palm. "Daddy's here, honey."

Marissa's heart flipped. Grady's love for his child was profound, and if she hadn't been sure that she was falling in love with him, it was confirmed when she watched him soothe his little girl—and when he'd held Marissa close and comforted her in the small hours of the morning. His strength had seeped through her as they'd kissed and she knew, right then, that she was in love with him. Wholly. Utterly. Irreversibly.

She offered to get him coffee and a sandwich from the café downstairs and came back fifteen minutes later carrying a small tray and found him in the same spot, eyes open, watching his baby girl sleep.

"My brother is coming a little later," he said and drank some coffee. "He's bringing me a change of clothes and some things for Tina. I also told him to grab one of Liz's dresses for you," he said and shrugged. "I hope that's okay."

"Sure," she replied. "I didn't realize you still had her things."

"I moved them into one of the spare rooms. I thought that when the girls were older they might want some of them." He shrugged again. "Maybe it's not such a good idea...you know, holding on to the past."

"She was their mother," Marissa said quietly. "I'm sure they'll appreciate it when they're old enough to understand."

"You're probably right."

The doctor arrived a few minutes later, and after checking Tina's temperature, she assured them that Tina was going to be fine.

"We'll keep her in for today and tonight and you can take her home tomorrow."

Marissa saw palpable relief on Grady's face. It was the best news they'd had in what felt like an eternity.

Tina slept off and on for the next couple of hours and Marissa returned to her chair by the window and watched silently as Grady sat by his daughter's bed, her tiny hand in his, talking to his child in a soft, low voice each time she stirred.

Brant arrived a few hours later. He dropped two small bags by the door, one for Tina and one for them, took one look at his older brother, tapped him on the shoulder and told him to get some rest. "You look shattered," Brant said and then nodded toward Marissa. "Go and get some sleep."

Grady shook his head. "I'm fine. And I'm not leaving."

Brant held up a hand. "She's out of danger now, right? I'm here and I'll stay until you get back. There's a hotel on this block. Go and get some rest for a few hours." He looked at Marissa again. "Both of you."

"He's probably right," she said softly. "You haven't slept and won't be able to drive her home tomorrow if you don't get some rest."

It took a couple more minutes to convince him, but finally he agreed. But only after Brant assured him that he'd call if anything changed. They both kissed a sleeping Tina, grabbed the bag of fresh clothes Brant had brought with him and left the hospital.

The afternoon sun was warm and Marissa blinked a few times to adjust to the different light when they reached the pavement outside. The parking lot was busy and she spotted Grady's truck easily. "We should walk," she said and turned right on the path.

"My truck is—"

"Walk," she said again. "I don't want you falling asleep at the wheel, even if it's a few hundred yards."

He rubbed his hand over his eyes, nodded and followed her.

The hotel had only a suite available, and he didn't quibble about the ridiculous price. Marissa followed Grady to the elevator without a word. The room was opulent and comfortable, with a kitchen, a lounge and two bedrooms—one with a king bed, the other with twin singles.

"I'll take the twin bedroom," Marissa said as she dropped her tote on the sofa while Grady placed the bag in the hall and then called his mother to check on his eldest daughters. He spoke to Colleen for several minutes, and when he ended the call he stretched his shoulders out and took a deep breath.

"The girls are okay. They're looking forward to having their sister home. It's been a long eighteen hours," he said.

She nodded. "Yes, it certainly has been. I'm so relieved that she's going to be all right. And you look exhausted," she said, taking in his weary expression, ruffled hair and five-o'clock shadow. "I don't know how you got through the night without sleeping."

He shrugged. "You didn't make out much better. And I would stay awake as long as I needed to for one of my children."

"I know you would," she said earnestly. "It makes you a great dad. Probably the best one I've ever known. Not that I have a lot of experience with fathers," she said with a rueful smile.

His mouth curled at the edges. "Then it has even more meaning." He paused for a moment, meeting her gaze. "I know you've missed having a father of your own, Marissa... but, you know, it might not be too late to change that. You could always try to find him."

She shook her head. "No. I wouldn't know where to start. And I wouldn't want to get my hopes up only to come to a dead end, so to speak. For all I know he's probably married with a family and I would just be one huge complication."

"But what if he's not?" Grady asked, his stare intense. "What if he wants exactly what you want? Connection? Family? What if he wants his daughter but isn't sure how she'll react if he reaches out?"

Marissa swallowed the heat in her throat. "It's a nice pipe dream. But he was a drifter, Grady. He doesn't even know I exist."

"But what if he did?"

She shrugged, feigning her disinterest. "It's all rather a moot point at this stage."

He stared at her and then shook his head. "I need a shower," he said. "Unless you'd like to go first?"

She waved her hand. "No…you go. The sooner you get into bed, the better."

It wasn't meant to sound intimate or provocative—but it did. His eyes glittered instantly and she knew he was as aware of the sudden heat between them as she was.

"You know, Marissa," he said softly, almost raspingly, "if you want to get me into bed, you only have to ask."

He turned on his heels and Marissa watched him walk down the narrow hall toward the bathroom. Her face burned with humiliation and she let out a deep, shuddering breath.

Jerk!

She sat on the sofa and twisted her hands together, silently cursing him.

And secretly loving him.

Grady had a way of finding her most vulnerable places. Her longing for a family, the pain she felt about her parentage…no one else made her think about it as he did. And he was right— she could try to find her father, but she was scared. Scared of who and what she'd find. Scared of knowing why he'd run off, to think he would reject her again. She'd had enough rejection in her life. Simon had discarded her without a second glance when he'd cheated on her.

All her life she'd felt the sting of being unwanted. She was an unplanned pregnancy to a seventeen-year-old girl barely out of high school. When her mother died, she experienced an acute abandonment that even living with her loving aunt Violet hadn't soothed. Only Liz had understood. Liz, with her five-star family and dreams of being a rancher's wife, who it turned out had lied to her about Grady's interest. But she didn't blame her friend. Liz had her own demons. Her own fears. The O'Sullivans had unrealistic expectations for their only daughter, and she knew Liz hadn't wanted the life they'd planned for her. She didn't want to go to college and become part of the great O'Sullivan moneymaking machine. She didn't want to be a trophy wife to some rich man who'd been handpicked for her by her parents. She'd wanted marriage to a man she truly loved and kids and happily-ever-after—which is exactly what she'd had...until she died.

Who am I to judge? I've fallen in love with my best friend's husband.

Marissa got to her feet and shook herself off. She walked up the hallway just as Grady opened the bathroom door—and then she stopped in her tracks.

He wore a towel draped around his hips and nothing else. Moisture clung to his skin, and as hard as she tried not to, her eyes moved over him appreciatively. Everything about him, every perfectly sculptured angle, was acutely masculine. The hair on his chest tapered down his belly and disappeared beneath the towel, and her fingers suddenly itched with the need to touch him, to trace her fingertips across his skin and mold her palms over the muscled contours of his chest.

She met his eyes and saw a kind of primitive, narcotic desire mirrored in his gaze. Longing coursed through her body, wholly and completely, making its way over her skin and through her blood. She'd never experienced anything like it, never knew she could want a man with such intensity. But she wanted Grady. And she knew he wanted her, too.

He moved and she waited for his touch, waited for him to take her into his arms, waited for him to say he wanted to make love to her. That he had to have her. That he loved her. But the words never came. He turned and opened the bedroom door. "Get some sleep, Marissa," he said flatly, shattering the mood between them as he stepped into the room and closed the door.

Then she hightailed it to the bathroom in five seconds flat.

She pressed her back against the door and sucked in a long breath.

What was she thinking? That Grady was actually going to fall in love with her? That he would return her feelings? He wanted her—that was all he'd said. She wasn't naive enough to imagine it could be anything more.

It's just a place to start...

His words echoed in her thoughts. A place to start, yes. But what? A real relationship? Or just an affair? And for how long? Until his desire for her was sated? Or did he want more? Was she crazy to think they could have a future together? He'd accused her of hiding behind Liz's memory to keep him at bay. And he was right.

Liz is gone...

He was right about that, too.

He'd said he would wait until she was ready. He wouldn't force. That wasn't his style. Despite the tense relationship they'd always had, Marissa knew he oozed honor. He was a man who lived by his word. A man who would always endeavor to do the right thing. He would never raise a hand in anger, never threaten or humiliate. He was honest and trustworthy and would always protect and cherish the people he cared about.

It was a seductive quality. Like catnip for her empty, lonely heart.

And Marissa suddenly knew exactly what she wanted.

Grady sat up in the bed, the sheet draped over his hips. He'd pulled the curtains together but the room was still light enough to make sleep impossible. He sent a text to his brother to ensure Tina was doing okay and waited for a reply. When that came a few seconds later, he placed his cell on the side table and took a few long, steadying breaths. He was just about to give sleep a try when there was a soft tap on the door.

"Come in."

The door opened and Marissa stood framed in the doorway. She wore a white toweling house robe that hung to her knees, her hair loose around her shoulders. His libido stirred instantly. Good manners told him to get up from the bed, but since he was naked, he was pretty sure she'd run like a scared rabbit if he did.

"Can I talk to you?" she asked, her voice barely a whisper.

Grady tugged at the sheet a little. "Sure."

She stepped into the room, arms crossed and eyes wide. "I wanted to make sure you were okay."

He frowned. "Why wouldn't I be?"

She shrugged. "I don't know…I guess I really wanted to say that I think I've been a little self-absorbed these past twelve hours. So, I'm sorry."

"Why would you think that?"

She shrugged a little. "You comforted me at the hospital when it should have been the other way around."

"You *were* comforting, Marissa," he said softly. "More than you know. And Tina's illness is not your fault. If anything, it's mine. I knew she was irritable and not herself these past few days. I should have figured out that she was unwell."

She crossed her arms. "Still, I shouldn't have fallen apart when you needed me to be strong. I guess I'm not good in a crisis."

"Sure you are. You were a tower of strength at Liz's funeral."

She took a deep breath. "I think I was so numb from grief I worked on a kind of autopilot that day."

"I wouldn't have gotten through it without you. Afterward, when we were alone, you were strong and comforting."

She sighed. "Grady…"

The anguished way she said his name almost tore him up inside. "What is it, Marissa?"

She bit her bottom lip. "Everything has changed so much."

"We haven't changed," he said softly. "We're still the same people we've always been. What's changed is how we feel about each other."

"Maybe," she said. "Only…I wish I could stop feeling so guilty."

"Guilty about what?" he asked, although he already knew.

"About this." She shuddered. "About you. Guilty because I want to stay here with you right now. Guilty because I want to lie down next to you and feel your arms around me."

Grady tensed and expelled a ragged breath. He was frustrated and turned on, and all he wanted to do was drag her onto the bed and kiss her beautiful mouth. But he didn't. "Guilt is a wasted emotion, Marissa. And Liz would never resent us being together."

"I'm not so sure," Marissa said quietly. "In senior year, just a few weeks before prom, I told her I hoped you would ask me to go. She told me you were seeing someone else. Then you started dating her. She asked me if I was okay with it… I said I was because I wanted her to be happy. We never spoke about it again, but I think she—"

"It was high school, Marissa," he said, cutting her off. "Kid stuff. And a lifetime ago. I can't tell you why Liz said what she did, and I can't and wouldn't want to go back and change anything. Because if I did it would mean that I wouldn't have my daughters and I wouldn't have had ten amazing years with my wife. But Liz is gone now. And we're right here…in this room…in this moment."

"In this moment?" she echoed, her voice hoarse. "In this moment I'm terrified of you."

Grady almost sprang out of bed. But he stayed where he was. "You have nothing to fear from me, Marissa. I'd never hurt you."

She shrugged again. "Perhaps not intentionally."

She was right; he would never intentionally hurt her. But he knew why she was resistant. "I know you've had a difficult time these past few years. I know you were married to a man who hit you, and that's probably made you wary of all men…but I would never do that."

"I know."

"Then why are you scared?"

She patted her chest. "In here I'm scared. I don't want to be hurt again."

Grady swallowed hard. He wasn't sure what to say. "I do care about you, Marissa."

She didn't respond and for a second he thought she was going to turn and run. But she didn't. She stepped closer to the bed, her hands resting on the belt around her waist. He watched and waited, and was so aroused he could barely think straight. The need to touch her amplified with each passing second and he groaned when she slowly tugged at the belt and the robe opened. She slipped it off her shoulders and it fell to the floor. And then she was naked, a perfect, divinely beautiful goddess.

The air rushed from his lungs. His gaze traveled over her slowly, absorbing everything, every dip, every valley. She was mesmerizing—her hair, her breasts, her hips, her long, smooth legs. Grady fought the urge to take her in his arms. He'd promised her it would be her call, her decision. So he'd wait. He'd pull on every ounce of self-control he possessed and let her take the lead.

Which she did.

He stayed perfectly still as she came to the bed and slid over him, resting a knee on each side of his hips. Grady held his breath as she pressed lower, straddling him in the most intimate way possible. She placed her hands on his shoulders and ran her palms down his chest. It was torture, but he still didn't touch her. He grabbed a handful of sheet in each hand, steadied himself and held her gaze.

And then she kissed him. Openmouthed, hot and erotic. Her tongue entwined with his and she sighed against his mouth. And he *still* didn't touch her. Her fingers moved over his chest slowly, killing him one touch at a time. Then her hands were in his hair, and as she pressed closer her breasts brushed against him. Her nipples were hard, grazing his as she moved, and when he could stand no more, Grady wrapped his arms around her, urging her even closer. And he kissed her, making love to her mouth just as he planned on making love to the rest of her.

Until he realized he didn't have a condom.

"Marissa," he groaned against her lips. "Birth control… I didn't…"

"I'm on the pill," she whispered, kissing him back as he grabbed her hips.

He nodded and trailed his mouth down her throat. Her

breasts were fuller than he'd imagined, and the pleasure he felt when he took her nipple into his mouth was almost overwhelming. He kept on kissing her, continued to return each kiss she bestowed. She moaned softly and pressed closer, and Grady pushed down the sheet that was still between them. He slid a hand between her legs and touched her and she almost bucked off the bed.

"Relax," he whispered and gently caressed her. She came apart in seconds, calling his name as she arched her back and moaned with pleasure. Grady kissed her again, over and over, deep, hot kisses that drove him wild. And then she moved over him, taking him inside her in a way that was so excruciatingly erotic he could barely draw breath into his lungs.

He held her hips as they moved together, felt the pressure slowly build as she thrust against him over and over until she climaxed again. And then he was gone, plummeting over the edge in a white-hot frenzy of release that was so intense for a second he thought he might pass out.

She collapsed against him, their ragged breathing the only sound in the dimly lit room.

"Oh…wow," she whispered into his chest.

"Yep," he said and took a deep breath. "That about covers it."

She giggled softly and met his gaze. "So much for sleeping."

"Sleeping is overrated," he said and quickly shifted their positions, holding her against him as he rolled and maneuvered until he was above her. "That's better."

"Control freak."

Grady smiled. "I thought I demonstrated quite a bit of self-control just now," he teased, loving how her skin flushed. "Although there was a whole lot of eagerness in what we just did and very little finesse. I'll do better next time."

"Next time?" Her brows rose and she ran her hands down his back. "And when is that, precisely?"

Laughter rumbled in his chest. "Oh, I'd say in about fifteen or twenty minutes."

"That's commitment."

"That's a promise."

And then he kissed her again and they spent the next three hours completely immersed in one another. He gave and he took and she did the same. Nothing intruded. No one could.

Marissa knew that the lack of sleep and three hours of making love with Grady would mean she'd probably need to hibernate for two days to recover from the fatigue. They managed to rest for an hour before they showered again and dressed in the clothes his brother had supplied. The long green dress with tiny white flowers on it was pure Liz, and as she slipped the garment over her hips, Marissa felt a familiar twinge of guilt press between her shoulder blades. Grady must have sensed her swift shift in mood, because he stopped what he was doing and spoke.

"Marissa…it's okay. It's just a dress."

She looked at him, with his shirt open, his feet bare, his stubble making him look sexier than any man had a right to look—it was impossible to regret what had happened between them. Because she loved him. There was no denying it. No avoiding it. He didn't love her back, of course. But he'd wanted her, *needed* her in the few hours they'd spent together.

They returned to the hospital at around seven o'clock that evening and Grady seemed remarkably chipper for a man who hadn't slept for nearly forty-eight hours.

Brant was in Tina's room and the toddler was awake and laughing at something her uncle had said and squealed loudly when her father came toward her. Marissa's heart rolled over as Tina bolted up in bed and stretched out her arms. She couldn't quell the tide of emotion that filled her eyes with tears. Seeing him with Tina made her long for a child of her own. A child with Grady.

The idea was suddenly overwhelming. She blinked a couple of times and excused herself, dashing from the room to find solace in the corridor.

"Marissa?" A deep voice said her name a minute or so later. "Are you okay?"

It was Brant. So serious, his handsome face was marred with a frown. She managed a tight smile and sniffed. "I'm fine...just overtired."

Brant nodded. "Fair enough. Grady asked me to drive you home. So, when you're ready to go, let me know."

He wants me to go home? He doesn't want me here...

It hurt through to her bones. Marissa nodded vaguely and then pulled herself together. She didn't want Grady's brother seeing her tears. The last thing she wanted was someone working out that she'd fallen hopelessly in love with Grady Parker.

She walked back into the room, back straight, and looked him directly in the eyes.

"Everything all right?" he asked.

"Fine," she replied and grabbed her tote from the chair.

Tina waved her arms and started chatting, and Marissa's chest tightened. She dropped the tote again and held out her arms, and the baby accepted her immediately. She experienced an intense surge of love for the little girl and hugged her close. Tina's small arms clung to her tightly, as though the toddler never wanted to let her go. And then she said something that pierced Marissa directly through the heart.

"Momma."

There was no other sound in the room. Just that one word, echoing around the walls.

Marissa instantly met Grady's gaze. He looked stunned, as though he couldn't quite believe what he'd just heard. And Marissa felt that way, too. She cuddled Tina for a little while longer and then reluctantly handed the baby back to him and grabbed her bag.

"I'm ready to go," she said to Brant, who was adjusting his collar and looked about as uncomfortable as anyone could. He nodded and then she looked at Grady. "Goodbye."

He didn't respond. He only looked at her. Into her. Through her. Tina chatted, oblivious to the sudden tension in the room. And it wasn't until Brant cleared his throat that Marissa moved her legs. She hugged her tote close to her hip, managed a weak smile and walked out.

The trip back to Cedar River was quiet, and she was glad Brant Parker wasn't the talkative type. Forty minutes later Brant pulled up outside her house and she politely thanked him for the ride. Once she was inside, Marissa took a shower, changed into her comfiest pale pink sweats and curled up on the sofa with a toasted cheese sandwich and a mug of soup. It was late, but she was hungry, and since her sleep patterns were off the charts anyway, she didn't think it mattered. It wasn't as if she had anything to wake up early for.

As it turned out she woke up at nine the following morning, feeling sluggish and stiff, no doubt a legacy from the aerobic workout she'd had between the sheets with Grady the previous afternoon. She dressed, grabbed her keys and headed into town to see Aunt Violet. But as she walked down the hospital corridor, she was stunned to see Rex coming out of her aunt's room.

He nodded but immediately looked uncomfortable. "Miss Ellis."

"Hello," she said, remembering that the last time they'd spoken had been at the renaming day, while they'd danced. And again, there was something about Rex that unsettled her. Not exactly in a bad way…it was something almost inexplicable. She couldn't define it. Couldn't make sense of it, either. And wasn't sure she wanted to. "Are you visiting my aunt?"

He held his hat tight against his chest and nodded. "Just payin' my respects."

Marissa met his brown-eyed gaze. "I wasn't aware you were that well acquainted," she said and then remembered how Aunt Violet had seemed disapproving when Marissa had mentioned how Rex had helped in her yard a couple of weeks earlier. "But you do know each other?"

"A little," he replied. "Well, I'll be seein' you."

He began to walk away but she said his name. "Rex…is there something going on I should know about?"

"Nothin', miss," he said, his eyes crinkling in the corners. "You take care."

He walked off and Marissa waited until he'd disappeared around the corner before she headed into her aunt's room. Violet was sitting in a chair by the window, her leg propped up. And she was frowning, as though she was seriously unhappy.

"Rex Travers was just here," Marissa said as she walked into the room. "Why?"

Violet shrugged. "You'll have to ask him."

"I did," Marissa said and sat in the chair opposite. "He said he was paying his respects."

"So, there you have it," her aunt said and grabbed a magazine from the coffee table beside her chair. "I hear Grady's little girl was unwell?"

"Yes," Marissa replied. "But I believe she's coming home from the hospital today."

Violet's expression softened. "You were with him at the hospital?"

She nodded. "Yes."

Her aunt sighed. "Are you getting involved there?"

Marissa shrugged. She didn't know what she was…at least, not to Grady. He'd sent her away. They'd made love, they'd connected in the most intimate way possible…and then he sent her home. It hurt so much she ached inside. "Maybe."

Violet smiled gently. "Just be careful. Three little girls will be a hard situation to walk away from if it doesn't work out."

Her stomach rolled over. The memory of Tina calling her *Momma* was impossible to forget. "I'll be careful. I promise."

She left the hospital after lunch, picked up a few groceries and got home around two. Once she put away her shopping, she changed into old jeans and a T-shirt, took some time feeding and brushing down Ebony and then spent an hour clearing out the first of the old greenhouses. She hauled old vines into piles out front and pulled out endless feet of plastic hose line that had been set up as a watering system.

It was after four when she took a break and was walking out of the greenhouse when she spotted a vehicle pulling up outside the house. Grady's pickup. She watched as he got out and headed up to the house. He knocked and waited on the porch and then headed back down the steps after a couple of minutes. It took him about ten seconds to scan the surroundings and see her by the greenhouse.

He strode across the yard and came to a halt about five feet in front of her. He looked so good. So familiar. But he looked tired, too. Like a man with a lot on his mind. His gaze was blistering, his hands tightly clenched. Twenty-four hours earlier she'd been making love with him. Now there was so much angst between them she could barely breathe. And then he spoke.

"We need to talk."

Chapter Ten

She had dirt on her face, she was frowning and she looked as if he was the last person she wanted to see...but still, Grady thought he'd never seen a more beautiful woman in his life. And she was glaring at him—her brown eyes were deep and rich and filled with fire.

She dropped the small pitchfork in her hand. "You didn't want to talk last night."

"Last night?" he echoed and stepped closer.

"You sent me packing."

Grady frowned. "Don't be ridiculous. I asked my brother to take you home because you looked exhausted."

Her hands came to her hips. "So now I'm ridiculous? Admit it, you asked your brother to take me home because you didn't want to deal with what happened between us. And then when Tina called me—"

"I asked Brant to take you home because I was concerned about you," he said, cutting her off, frustrated. "And as for not wanting to deal with what *happened*...which I assume you mean the fact that we made love yesterday, I absolutely want to deal with it, Marissa. In fact, I want to talk about it this very minute and work out what the hell we're supposed to do now."

She flinched and Grady took a hesitant step forward. Her chest heaved. Her eyes were boring into him. She looked beautiful and sexy, and all he wanted to do was haul her into his arms and kiss her provocative and tempting mouth.

"And as for what Tina said…" His words trailed off for a moment. "She's never had a mother. She's never felt that bond or that connection. Other than my own mother, you're the only woman she's spent considerable time with, so I'm not surprised she's latched on to you. But I'm sorry if it upset you."

She inhaled heavily, as if she had the weight of the world on her shoulders, and he fought the urge to take her into his arms. "It didn't upset me. I thought it upset *you*."

"Why would you think that?"

She shrugged. "Because…because things have changed so much. And because it would make it seem like I was replacing Liz, somehow. And I'm not," she added quickly. "I couldn't. I wouldn't."

What did she mean? That she didn't want to be around his daughters? Or him?

"I'm not looking to replace Liz," he said soberly. "Not in my eyes or in my kids' eyes. But you're right, things have changed and we can never go back to how things were. And frankly, I don't want to. So how about we just see where it goes from here?"

Her head tilted. "Is this about you wanting to date me again?"

"Why not?" he shot back. "You're not seeing anyone else, are you?"

"Well…no. But—"

"Neither am I," he said, cutting her off again. "So, why don't we date?"

"Are you crazy?" She shook her head. "What would people say?"

"What people?"

She flapped her arms. "I don't know, *people*. Like the O'Sullivans, for instance."

"I couldn't care less what the O'Sullivans think of me."

"Come on, Grady," she said with a groan. "You know that's not entirely true. And if we started dating, they'd be all over it like white on rice."

He laughed. Sometimes she had a flair for the dramatic. "I think that's overreacting."

She shook her head. "People would... People *might* think that we've been *seeing* one another the whole time."

"The whole time?" He stopped and thought about what she meant. "Hang on...are you saying you're worried people might say we were having an affair while Liz was alive?"

"Yes," she said tightly. "Exactly."

"Well, that's ludicrous, Marissa. No one would believe it."

"Wouldn't they? I think they would. And the O'Sullivans hate you enough already without adding fuel to the fire."

"Why this sudden concern for my reputation?" he asked. "Or is it a convenient way of avoiding the inevitable?"

"Inevitable?"

"Yeah," he said and grabbed her hand. "You and me. Inevitable."

"Nothing is inevitable," she shot back. "I'm not going to date you, Grady."

"You know," he said and caressed her fingertips, "lovers tend to date one another."

She pulled her hand away and stepped back. "I'm not going to be your lover, either."

"It's too late for that. We're already lovers, Marissa," he said softly. "And that first time…it was incredible."

He saw her cheeks spot with color, and it made him smile. After everything, she could still blush. "It was a mistake."

Grady sighed. There was enough finality in her voice that he figured he needed another angle. "The girls want to see you. Why don't you come to the ranch tomorrow afternoon and we'll drive into town for a pizza."

She frowned. "That sounds like a date."

He shrugged, feigning innocence. "No. If it was a date, I'd take you somewhere much swankier than JoJo's Pizza Parlor. I'd take you to dinner and then dancing and then we'd probably make out for a bit in the parking lot and then I would take you home and make love to you slowly all night long."

Just the idea of it sent blood rushing to his groin. "But since it's only to be JoJo's Pizza Parlor, you'll have three chaperones and will be perfectly safe. See you tomorrow, around five," he said and turned before she had opportunity to refuse.

She should have simply stayed home. But the idea of disappointing Breanna, Milly and Tina was too much to bear. She dressed in her favorite jeans, a hot-pink shirt, a white sweater and her fancy boots. She left her hair loose, didn't bother with her contact lenses and headed off at ten minutes to five.

The baby was getting bathed when she arrived, so Breanna and Milly let her in. When she stuck her head around the bathroom door, she saw Grady kneeling on the floor, covered in water and bubbles, and a wailing Tina clearly not happy about getting her hair washed. Her sisters were laughing from the doorway as Grady pulled the toddler from the tub and wrapped her in a towel.

He looked up and smiled when he saw her, and her heart just about burst through her chest. Boy, he sure had a killer smile. And he looked sexy as sin with his hair and shirt wet.

And then I would take you home and make love to you slowly all night long...

A girl could melt hearing words like that. She'd tried not to think about it...and had failed big-time.

Tina held out her arms when she saw Marissa. "Shall I take over?" she asked.

"She's all yours," he said with a grin and passed Tina over. "She's been acting up all afternoon. And asking for you."

"She looks so much better," Marissa said as she was covered in butterfly kisses from the toddler.

"Yes. She's almost her usual self. A bit cranky still," he said and touched his daughter's head gently. "But getting better all the time. Her clothes are on her bed." He looked down at his wet shirt and jeans. "I'll just get changed."

Marissa spent a fun ten minutes getting Tina ready. Breanna and Milly were already dressed, so they came into the room and chatted as she got their sister into her clothes and shoes. Grady appeared in the doorway a little while later, dressed in dark jeans and a pale blue chambray shirt that showed off every asset he possessed. The girls were racing around begging for pizza, Tina was demanding she take her favorite stuffed animal and Marissa could only look into Grady's eyes.

"Ready to go?" he asked.

She nodded and hauled Tina onto her hip, then grabbed her tote, which she'd left by the front door.

When they arrived at JoJo's, they were seated almost immediately. The restaurant was a popular one for families, with its long tables and red-checked cloths. Ordering was fun and after much pleading he relented and ordered small sodas for Breanna and Milly and large ones for himself and Marissa. The kids munched on the tiny bread sticks in the center of the table while they waited for their food.

"You know," he said once their drinks had arrived and the girls' attention was taken over with their soda and the bread, "you look cute in glasses."

Marissa touched the frames. "Do I look smarter?"

"You're the smartest woman I've ever met."

She laughed. "Then you haven't met many women."

"I've met enough," he said so softly, so silkily that her cheeks flared with heat.

She didn't want to think about him and other women. "Well…thanks for the compliment. I'm giving my imperfect vision a break from contact lenses for a day or so."

"There's nothing imperfect about you, Marissa."

It was a good line. He could flirt with the best of them, that was for certain. She laughed softly. "Maybe it's you who needs glasses."

He chuckled. "I see just fine. So, have you decided to buy the farm from your aunt?"

She shrugged loosely. "I'm not sure. Maybe… I mean, it was my home for a long time after my mother died. And since it used to be a working vegetable farm, I could think about growing *something*. But if I did, I'd need to research about local growers and potential markets. I have a long way to go, of course, since I know nothing about growing vegetables." She smiled and shrugged. "So I consider myself a work in progress."

He stared at her. "Do you miss it?" he asked suddenly. "Your old life? Your career?"

Her mouth twisted thoughtfully. "Less than I imagined I would. I certainly don't miss the *life*," she added. "I mean, I had a few friends in New York, but most of them stayed friendly with my ex-husband. As for the work, I enjoyed it well enough and I always considered I was good at it. But it was never a real calling. It was something I did after college."

"You switched majors midway through college. Why?"

She shrugged again. "I guess I didn't think I could make a living out of my craft. I mean, I love potting, I love creating pieces and seeing the stages from clay to the final result…but Aunt Violet always wanted me to do something else and I—"

"What did *you* want to do?"

"Honestly," she said on a sigh, "I think I always believed I'd work for a few years and then get married and have a family. That just wasn't the way it turned out."

"It's not too late, though," he said quietly, his gaze narrowing. "You're only thirty-two."

She shrugged. "I guess."

She was dying inside. She didn't want to talk to Grady about marriage and babies. He wanted to *date* her. That was all. Nothing more. Dating and sex. It was as bad as friends with benefits. What she dreamed of…what she wanted…was *romance*. The whole sappy, romantic fairy tale. She wanted it all…flowers, chocolate, wooing…a real, bona fide courtship. One that ended in an even sappier marriage proposal. Simon's proposal had been swift and serious and as if he was closing a business deal. There certainly hadn't been any flowers or wooing involved. They'd married in a swift civil ceremony with only Liz and Grady and a few friends as witnesses, and she'd worn a sensible cream dress. No flowers or confetti, that was for certain. Those kinds of trappings were ridiculous, according to her ex-husband. Next time— *if* she had a next time—she wanted things to be different.

It sounded foolish just thinking about it. But the heart wanted what the heart wanted.

Their pizzas arrived and she was glad for the reprieve.

The girls ate with gusto and she laughed at how much sauce Milly got on her face and in her lap. Breanna proudly consumed two large pieces and Tina picked the cheese off her piece and tossed the pepperoni at her father. It was a fun evening for Marissa, even though she felt the underlying thread of tension between herself and Grady. Which she figured couldn't be helped. They'd crossed a line by sleeping together. There was no going back from sex. It was done. All she had to do was find a way to forget about it and move on.

"Great."

Grady's voice cut through her thought. "What is it?" she asked.

He slanted his gaze toward the front of the restaurant. "Liam O'Sullivan."

Marissa glanced around and spotted the eldest O'Sullivan son waiting by the front counter, obviously picking up takeout. He was watching them and frowning, and by his expression, clearly making a judgment.

"Oh, God," she said in a low voice so the girls couldn't hear. "I'm sorry, Grady. You know what he's going to think, that this is a date, and he'll probably go and tell—"

"It is a date," he said, cutting her off. "And he can tell whoever he likes."

Marissa's eyes widened. "You don't care."

Grady shook his head. "Not one bit."

By the time they got back to the ranch, it was nearly eight-thirty. The girls were all sleepy, and while Grady put Tina down for the night she stayed with Breanna and Milly while they swapped their clothes for pajamas and hopped into bed. She read them a story and then another and waited on the small seat by Milly's bed for Grady to come back to tuck them in. When he came into the room and sat on the edge of Breanna's bed, Marissa excused herself and walked out, lingering in the hall outside.

"Daddy?" she heard his daughter speak.

"Yes, Breanna?"

"Milly and I have been thinking."

Milly giggled at the sound of her name and it made Marissa smile.

"Thinking about what?" Grady asked.

Breanna, so serious and sometimes stern, spoke quietly. "That we'd like to have a new mommy," she announced, so serenely innocent it tugged at Marissa's heart.

Grady cleared his throat a little. "Well, honey, I—"

"And if you married Marissa, she'd be our new mommy," Breanna said, and Milly cheered from the other side of the room. "And that's what we want more than anything."

Not a pin dropping...

That's all Marissa could think as Breanna's announcement resonated around the room and then down the hall.

The blood rushed from her face and she gave a tiny gasp.

She waited for him to gently tell his daughter that it was impossible. That people got married only when they were in love with each other, or something else that she might understand. But he didn't. He said something else.

"I'll...I'll see what I can do, okay?"

Breanna giggled. "Yay! But hurry, Daddy," the child said, serious again. "Just in case she marries someone else."

"I don't think you need worry about that."

His blasé words were enough to quickly get her to her feet. She went back in to say good-night to the girls, gave them each a kiss and left the room. By the time she reached the living room, she was shaking so badly she had to perch herself on the sofa.

I don't think you need worry about that...

She felt like sobbing for all eternity. Was she so far

from marriage material? Insensitive, unfeeling jerk! Grady came into the room a few minutes later, and there was more silence…this time thicker and hotter. She summoned all the strength she could and sucked in a long, steadying breath.

"How could you do that?"

He shrugged. "Do what?"

"I'll see what I can do?" she reminded him. "What did that mean?"

He was frowning. "I was only—"

"Go back in there and tell them," she demanded, springing to her feet. "Go and tell them that it's impossible. Go and tell them that you made a mistake and shouldn't have said it. Go and tell them or I'll—"

"No," he said, cutting her off. "You heard them, Marissa. It's what they want."

She wanted to clamp her hands to her ears and drown out the sound of his deep, seductive voice. She wanted to stop her heart from pounding like a jackhammer in her chest.

"But it's not what I want."

His head tilted fractionally. "No? Which part? Being their mother?" he asked and came farther into the room. "Or being my wife?"

"Don't do that," she said hotly. "Don't make me out to be the bad guy here. You know this is impossible."

He shrugged. "My daughters have asked me for something. And it's something I can give them. Why would I think that's impossible?"

Marissa gave him a death stare. "Because…because it just is. Yesterday you said you wanted to *date* me," she reminded him. "And now you're saying you want to *marry* me?"

He shrugged again. "I'm saying that my children have asked me to give them a mother, and I'll do whatever I have to do to make them happy."

Humiliation coursed across her skin. It sounded as if he was making some kind of supreme sacrifice. If she didn't love him, she would have hated him in that moment.

"Even if it makes you *unhappy*?"

"But it wouldn't," he said quietly. "We get along, you love my daughters and we're great in bed together. We could make this work, Marissa."

They got along and had great sex. He'd lost his mind—it was the only answer. "I married the wrong man once. I'm not going to make the same mistake again."

He scowled and then his cheeks slashed with color. "Seriously? You're comparing me to that lowlife you were married to?"

"No, of course not," she said quickly. "But I know what a bad marriage tastes like, Grady. And I don't want another one. And sex isn't enough to hold two people together."

"What about three little girls who adore you?" he shot back. "Would that be enough?"

She wished it was. She wished it more than anything. But Marissa knew that wishes were for fools. He didn't love her. He never would. He might care; he'd even told her as much only days earlier. But caring wasn't loving. And lukewarm affection and great sex would never be enough to sustain a marriage.

She pulled her keys from her tote and rattled them. "Look, I understand why you think you have to make this offer. I love the girls, too…and I want them to be happy. But not like this."

He stood perfectly still. "Tonight you said you wanted to get married and have a family. Well, I'm offering you exactly that, Marissa. There are three little girls down the hall longing for a mother's love. You can have that and a baby or two of your own when you're ready. And you'll also have a faithful husband. What's the problem?"

You're the problem...

If she wasn't so hurt, she would have said so. God, it was worse than Simon's proposal. Grady Parker possessed all the romance and sensitivity of a rock.

"I have to go."

"Marissa," he said her name on a seductive breath. "We can make this work. Just say you'll think about it, okay?"

She nodded, her heart breaking. It sounded so perfect. So easy. Too easy.

"Good night, Grady."

Then she left.

"You did *what?*"

Grady was at the Loose Moose Tavern with Brant on Wednesday afternoon. Months ago the place had been partially gutted by fire, and his foolish little brother had gone and bought the building with plans to renovate and reopen it as a tavern with a restaurant and bar. The only good thing about the plan was how ticked off the O'Sullivans would be about the idea. He kicked at a small pile of burned timber and swiveled on his heels.

"You heard," he said and crossed his arms.

Brant's eyes widened. "And she turned you down?"

"Yep."

"Harsh," Brant said. "Did she give you a reason?"

"She gave me plenty."

His brother smiled. "And do you plan on going back for more?"

He shrugged. "My kids want Marissa. She's all they want."

"And what do you want?"

Grady let out a long, weary breath. "I liked being married. I liked having someone to talk to. I miss that. And I'm tired of sleeping alone." His brother grinned at his words and Grady frowned. "I was happy—you should try it sometime. It might make you less disagreeable."

Brant laughed. "Not a chance. Does Mom know?"

Grady groaned. "No…and don't say anything."

"I won't," his brother assured him. "I'm staying away from Mom and that Cupid's arrow of hers."

"She did promise you were next," Grady said and laughed.

They stayed at the tavern for another half hour and then Grady bailed to do a few errands and leave enough time to pick up the girls from school. He stopped by his mother's to collect Tina about an hour before he needed to be at the school and was surprised to see Marissa's car out front. He hadn't been near her for days. And she hadn't contacted him. There was another car parked outside, an old Honda Civic. Inside he found his mother, Marissa and Lucy Monero sitting at his mom's kitchen table, drinking tea and laughing. Marissa glanced at him over her glasses and then quickly looked away. Tina was in Marissa's lap, playing with her watch and bangle. He liked seeing them together, liked knowing how much his children meant to her.

Even if she won't marry me…yet.

The more he considered it, the more it made sense. Marissa was exactly what he needed. She was one of the few people he trusted with his kids. And she loved them as they loved her. It was the perfect solution. His daughters needed a mother. And he needed a wife…despite how much he'd vetoed the idea over the past year. The last thing Liz had said to him was to be happy, and out of loyalty he'd stayed faithful to her memory. But he needed more than memories to give his daughters the life they deserved. They'd told him what they wanted and Grady would do whatever it took to give it to them. They wanted Marissa. And he wanted her, too.

His mother looked up guiltily when he entered the room, and he would have bet his boots that they had been talking about him. Lucy quickly explained that she'd dropped by to see how Tina was doing, and Marissa stayed silent, seemingly immersed in chatting to his daughter. But Grady wasn't fooled. The awareness between them throbbed with a will of its own. It had been building for weeks and now he could no longer deny it. And he was determined to make her see that marrying him was the best solution for them all.

"You're later than I expected," his mother said.

"I've been at the Loose Moose with Brant."

"Colleen was telling us how he's bought the place," Lucy said and smiled. "It's an ambitious project."

"Damned foolish idea if you ask me," he said and grinned. "But he's determined."

"You should drop over and see the place," his mom said to Lucy, and Grady suppressed a chuckle. He knew that look in his mother's eye. Pure matchmaker. He made a mental note to warn his brother next time they spoke. Then again, Lucy Monero was a pretty, friendly and successful doctor and Brant did spend too much time alone…so what harm could it do?

"Well, I should get going," Marissa said. "I promised Aunt Violet I'd drop by this afternoon." She kissed Tina's head and propped her on the chair and then collected her bag.

"We'll come with you," Grady said quickly and scooped his daughter up. "I'm sure Miss Violet would like a visit from Tina."

He saw his mother's curious expression and promptly ignored it. She had better things to do now she'd set her sights on Brant hooking up with Lucy Monero. He thanked his mother for babysitting, said farewell to Lucy, grabbed

Tina's things and headed outside. Marissa was already by her car and he shuffled Tina on his hip as he walked toward her.

"I'll meet you over there," he said. "It'll only be a short visit as I have to pick the girls up from school."

She looked annoyed. "I thought you were getting a new housekeeper to help with all that."

He shrugged. "I've interviewed a few but none were suitable."

"Maybe you expect too much."

"Maybe," he agreed. "Anyhow, it's not really a housekeeper I need. Or want."

She glared, because she knew exactly what he meant. "I'll see you at the hospital."

They pulled up in the hospital parking lot at the same time and he was surprised that she waited for him before heading inside. Tina raced up and grabbed Marissa's hand and Grady realized he'd been usurped. But he didn't mind. Marissa was good for his kids. He just had to get her to realize that, too.

He was about to head into the building when he spotted Rex's old pickup in the lot. What was *he* doing here? Grady's gut dipped. Was Rex sick? Was that why he was at the hospital? He'd told the other man to tell Marissa the truth about her parentage and knew that hadn't happened yet. He didn't know what was holding Rex back. Sure, Marissa would be shocked, but he was certain she'd understand and eventually welcome her father into her life. But if he was sick? That made things a whole lot more complicated.

"So, how have you been?" he asked as casually as he could.

"Fine."

"I thought I'd come around on Saturday about nine and give you a riding lesson."

She started walking up the path. "Under what conditions?"

"No conditions," he said and grinned. "Just being neighborly."

"Said the wolf to the lamb."

Grady laughed. "Rest assured, I have no ulterior motive in wanting to teach you how to ride. Except," he said and grasped her free hand, "in getting you to agree to marry me."

She pulled free and scowled. "You're unbelievable."

He grinned. "Incidentally, I talked to Breanna and Milly again this morning and they're all for it. All we need to do is get a license and set the date."

She kept walking. "You clearly have a hearing problem. I said no. I meant no."

"We could do it at the courthouse," he suggested, ignoring her protests. "Tanner and Cassie got married there a few months back."

He saw her scowl, watched her shoulders go back and knew she was madder than hell. They entered through the hospital doors and swung left toward the small rehab ward where her aunt was staying. Tina was holding her hand, walking compliantly beside her, and it only amplified his need to get her agreement. His kids needed Marissa. And he needed Marissa. As he needed air in his lungs or ground beneath his feet. He wanted to marry her and raise his daughters with her and one day feel her belly filled with their child.

Because...

Because he was in love with her.

Completely and crazily in love with her.

She was in his heart and soul and he loved her more

than he'd imagined he could ever love anyone again. The realization rocked him to the core and he stopped walking. He took a deep breath and watched as she headed down the corridor, his little girl at her side. Emotion clogged his throat and love swept over him like a wave. And he wanted to tell her, right then and there. He wanted to ask her to love him in return.

"Marissa?"

She was twenty feet away but had stopped walking and was outside her aunt's room. When she turned her head back to look at him, Grady saw a kind of wary shock, even despair on her face.

"What's wrong?"

She was shaking her head, and Tina, as though somehow sensing something wasn't right, remained silent at Marissa's side. Grady reached her in a few long strides, came to an abrupt halt and took his daughter's hand.

And then he understood.

Voices were coming from the room.

Miss Violet and Rex.

"And I just don't think now is the right time," Violet said, clearly frustrated.

"Then when will it be the right time?" Rex shot back. "I've been waiting six years. Six long years, Violet. She has a right to know."

Grady saw Marissa's expression shift to suspicion and he immediately wanted to spare her what he knew was coming. She met his gaze, almost pleadingly, as she began to shake her head.

"Not yet," Violet said. "Marissa's been through enough these past couple of years and if you tell her now it will only—"

"I don't want to hurt her. I just want to be a part of her

life. Whatever you think, she's my daughter, Violet," Rex said, and Marissa's gasp echoed down the hall.

The talking stopped, and before he could stop her, Marissa bolted into the room. By the time he moved through the doorway, Marissa was already demanding answers.

"What did you say?" She shot the question directly to Rex.

The older man looked at her despairingly. And then he spoke. "I've been wanting to tell you for a while… I'm your father, Marissa."

Marissa shook her head. "That's crazy." She looked at her aunt. "Aunt Violet, tell me that this isn't—"

"It is true," Violet said, tears in her eyes. "Rex Travers *is* your father."

Marissa was still shaking her head, still looking as if she couldn't believe what she had heard. Finally, she glanced toward Grady. She wanted reassurance. Support. She wanted it contradicted. But he slowly nodded.

Everyone looked shattered. Except for Tina, who demanded attention, and Grady quickly lifted the toddler into his arms. Then took a step closer to Marissa.

"How about we go and—"

"You knew?"

He couldn't miss the accusation in her voice. The disbelief. The suspicion.

"Marissa…"

She backed up a few steps. "You knew and you didn't tell me?"

Guilt pressed down on his shoulders. "I couldn't tell you."

"How long?" she asked. "How long have you known?"

He sighed. "A couple of weeks."

She took another step back. "You've known this for weeks and you didn't say anything?" she asked, firmer, harder.

"After everything we…" Her words quickly disappeared and he could feel her pain with every fiber in his body.

Then she turned and left. Out of the room. Out of sight.

And away from everyone he knew she thought had betrayed her.

Including him.

Chapter Eleven

Broken and betrayed. That's how she felt. That's how she'd felt for forty-eight hours. Everyone had called her. Aunt "I should have told you sooner" Violet. Rex "father of the year" Travers. Grady "big fat liar" Parker.

Grady had come to the house twice. He'd knocked on the door and hung out on the steps for ten minutes each time until he'd finally gotten the message and left. Marissa had stayed resolute. She didn't want to see anyone. She didn't want to talk about *it*. She wanted to be left alone. And she didn't want to hear excuses or explanations. She'd heard enough.

Mid-morning on Friday she went into town and did some grocery shopping and then headed to the feed store and arranged for some hay to be delivered for Ebony. Afterward she hung around outside the hospital with every intention of visiting Aunt Violet but couldn't bring herself to go inside at first. She circled the lobby for twenty minutes and then finally summoned the courage to go into her aunt's room.

Violet was by the bed, propped up in a chair, a bag by her feet that she was slowly filling with items from the small chest of drawers next to the bed. She looked up when Marissa entered the room and smiled.

"It's good to see you," her aunt said.

"You, too," she said and sat down by the window. "You're packing?"

"Yes. Moving to another part of the rehab ward tomorrow, and in a week I should be ready to move permanently."

"Wonderful," she said and looked out the window. "I've started clearing out the old greenhouses and—"

"I know you're angry, Marissa," her aunt said, cutting through her words. "So be angry."

"I'm not angry with you," she admitted. "I guess you have your reasons for not saying anything."

Violet nodded. "I did what I thought was right for you. When he reappeared in town six years ago, I knew it wouldn't be too long before he found out about you. All he had to do was ask around about Janie and he'd quickly discover she'd had a daughter. I didn't expect him to stay, though. I thought he'd disappear like he had last time."

Emotion burned her throat. "So he never knew my mom was pregnant?"

"No," Violet replied. "By the time Janie found out, he was long gone. He was a transient, Marissa. A good-looking cowboy with barely a dime in his pocket who moved around from town to town, looking for work when he could get it. And he just happened to be passing through this town when Janie caught his eye. And then a couple weeks later he left."

It sounded sordid. No wonder her mother had never said anything about it. What child would want to hear that kind of story? Marissa had spent two days thinking about it and wondering what she should do next. But it was an easy decision. She'd never had a father. She still didn't.

"When he came back six years ago, what did he say to you?" she asked quietly.

"He said he was staying," Violet replied and sniffed. "He knew you came back a couple of times a year to visit me and Liz and the girls and said he hoped he'd get to see you during those times. Of course, I didn't agree with his decision, but there was little I could do about it."

Marissa sighed heavily. "I wish you'd told me this, Aunt Violet."

"I know," her aunt said. "I should have. I was wrong to keep the truth from you. I just wanted to protect you."

Marissa nodded. "I know you did."

She stayed for another ten minutes and then headed home. As she drove up the gravel driveway, she spotted Grady's truck parked outside her house and was almost tempted to turn around and head back into town. But since that was the coward's way, she sucked in a deep breath, drove into the driveway and parked beside the house.

Grady was on the steps and rose to his feet once she turned off the ignition. Marissa opened the trunk, grabbed the couple of grocery bags and then locked the car.

He was beside her in a second. "Here, give me those."

She shrugged past him and ignored his request. "Go away."

"I'm not going anywhere until we've talked," he insisted and followed her up the steps.

Marissa dumped the bags on the love seat by the door and rummaged in her tote for the house keys. She didn't want to look at him. Didn't want to think how safe and strong his arms seemed. She only wanted him to leave.

"Marissa?"

She turned on her heels. "I don't want to talk to you."

He sighed wearily. "Then would you at least talk to your father?"

"Don't call him that," she snapped and glared at him. "I don't have a father."

"Oh, yeah, you do," Grady said with annoying confidence. "And he wants to see you."

"Really?" Her brows rose. "Then why are you here instead of him?"

"He asked me to talk to you first, maybe smooth things over a little."

Marissa winced. Grady Parker was an emotional wrecking ball. "And how do you think that's going so far?"

"Would you please just listen?" he asked impatiently.

Marissa held out her hands. "Okay…I'm listening."

"He wants to have the chance to explain, to talk to you about his relationship with your mom."

"I know all about it," she said quietly. "Aunt Violet told me he was a drifter who came to town, got my mother pregnant and then left. And yes, I know he didn't know she was pregnant…but I can't see how that would have made any difference."

"He only wants a chance to talk with you," Grady said with a heavy sigh. "He's a good man, Marissa. And he stayed once he knew about you. He stayed in town and got a job working at the ranch. He knew Liz was your friend and figured that way he might get to see you sometimes."

"And stayed silent."

"That was your aunt's idea. She was looking out for you, that's all. If you could look past your temper and stop being stubborn for one minute, you would—"

"My temper?" She dropped the keys and her tote on the love seat. God, he was insufferable. "Is that what you think this is about? Me being angry with my aunt and Rex?"

"What else?"

"You," she shot back. "I'm angry with you. I feel hurt and betrayed and so mad at you for not telling me the truth."

"It wasn't my place."

"Your *place*?" she echoed incredulously. "It became your place the first time you kissed me. It became your place the moment we stepped into that hotel room last week. And it certainly became your place after that offensive marriage proposal."

"Offensive?"

Marissa let out a brittle laugh at his affronted tone. "What else would you call it? Oh, hang on… *I'll see what I can do.* I think that's how it went. You're about as romantic as a load of laundry."

His cheeks slashed with color. "Romance?" He said the word as if his mouth was full of broken glass. "Seriously?"

"What can I say?" she said and shrugged. "I'm a girl… I believe in all that stuff. And I want it. I want the flowers and the music and the poetic love notes and all of that sugary nonsense. I didn't have it the first time around. I married a man I hardly knew and ended up regretting it through to my bones. I married him because I was alone and lonely and thought it was time I got married. I settled. But I'm not going to settle again."

"You think you'd be *settling* if you married me?"

She nodded, hurting all over. "Yes."

His shoulders sagged slightly. "I see. I'll tell Rex to come by and talk to you in the next couple of days—if that's okay with you."

"Sure," she said vaguely. "Whatever."

He turned and walked down the steps with a kind of weary resignation that should have thrilled her. But didn't. He looked…defeated. But she was right to say what she did. A marriage without love on both sides *was* settling. And she wouldn't do it. She couldn't. Not even for the three little girls she loved so much. As he got into his truck and drove away, Marissa's eyes filled with tears, and once his pickup was out of sight she dropped onto the love seat and sobbed.

"Well, what did she say? Will she see me? Can I talk to her? Is she still angry?"

Grady wasn't even out of his truck before Rex started barking out questions.

He got out and slammed the door. "It's not you she's angry at."

Rex was frowning and then he half smiled, wrinkling his already weathered face. "She's mad at *you*?"

"Yeah."

"Why?" Rex asked. "What did you do?"

"Nothing…apparently."

The older man frowned again and Grady didn't hang around for any more questions. He headed inside and found his mother and brother in his kitchen. Both had seen fit to invite themselves over for dinner.

"Where are the girls?" he asked as he poured a cup of coffee he didn't want.

"Tina is having a nap and the other two are playing in their room," his mother replied, looking at him curiously. "You weren't gone long. I thought you had errands to do."

"I did what I went out for."

The door to the mudroom opened and Rex came barreling in through the open back kitchen door.

"You didn't answer my question," Rex said hotly, still scowling. "What did you do to my daughter?"

"Nothing," Grady assured him. "Go and see her in a day or so. She'll probably be ready to talk to you then."

"And you?"

Grady ignored the question and drank some coffee. "We've talked enough."

"Did you ask her again?"

Brant's voice this time. Interfering and way out of line. Grady scowled at his younger brother. "No. And don't start with—"

"Ask her what?" Colleen was all eyes and ears in her quest for details.

"Nothing," Grady replied.

"He asked Marissa to marry him," Brant supplied, so matter-of-factly Grady was tempted to punch him in the mouth.

"You did what?"

Colleen and Rex, simultaneously asking the same thing, looked as if their heads were going to explode.

"Can you keep your voices down?" Grady said, frowning. "I don't want the girls hearing this."

His mother nodded. "So, you proposed to Marissa?" she asked quietly.

"Yes, okay," Grady said irritably and poured the coffee down the sink. "I asked her to marry me. I asked Marissa to marry me and she refused." He glared at his younger brother. "Happy? Now that everyone knows I've made a complete fool out of myself over a woman who thinks she'd be *settling* if she was my wife!"

Grady quickly left the kitchen, took the few steps down to the mudroom and strode out of the house. He fought the hurt and rage climbing over his skin and took a few long breaths to calm himself as he walked across the yard and toward the stables. He grabbed the saddle, bridle and blanket and headed for Solo's stall. The big paint gelding snickered when he undid the bolt on the door, and a few minutes later the horse was tacked up and Grady was in the saddle.

He stayed out for about an hour, riding along the fence line, determined to get the anger out of his belly. Solo had a rhythmic, easy canter, and with the feel of the breeze on his face and the sound of the gelding's hooves pounding over the grass, it gradually eased the hot ache he felt all over.

Marissa...

He said her name to the wind and hoped it would be cathartic.

But he still hurt all over. He still felt like a fool. He still didn't know how to stop wanting her.

By the time he returned to the stables, it was past three o'clock. He walked Solo into the stable, pulled off the saddle and bridle and brushed him down.

"So, you get all that out of your system?"

Brant was by the door, elbows rested on the stall.

"Just about," he replied and tossed the curry comb in the bucket.

"Do you want to talk about it?"

"About Marissa? No, thanks," Grady said and grabbed the hay net off the wall. He left the stall for the feed room and returned a minute later with the net filled with grassy hay. His brother hadn't moved. "You're still here?"

"Yep. Mom sent me to talk to you."

Grady laughed humorlessly. "Really. You? Talking?"

Brant shrugged loosely. "So I'm more of a listener than a talker."

"Then go and listen to Mom tell you all about Lucy Monero," Grady said. "That should have you bailing in about two seconds flat."

Brant managed a good-humored scowl. "We're not talking about me. This is about you and Marissa."

"There's nothing to talk about," he shot back. "She turned me down. She doesn't want me. She doesn't want the girls. She doesn't want to *settle*. She wants music and flowers and poetic love notes."

"What?" Brant asked, frowning.

"You heard. That's what she said she wants."

"Isn't that what all women want?" Brant tapped his fingertips on the door and looked at him. "So, you're in love with her, then?"

Heat crept up his neck and he shrugged. "Stupid, huh?"

His brother half smiled. "Well, you've always been the sentimental one."

"But not romantic," he said quietly. *Flowers. Music. Love notes.* It was ridiculous. They weren't eighteen. High school was over. He was a grown man with three children and he wasn't going to get distracted by silly romantic nonsense. Besides, she'd made her feelings abundantly clear. Egotistical he wasn't, but that didn't mean he was going to keep pursuing a woman who thought she'd be *settling.* Only an idiot would do that. "You going to crash here tonight?"

"Sure," Brant said.

"Good. Can you watch the girls for me in the morning and then drop them off at Mom's?"

"If you like. Where are you going?" his brother asked.

"I promised Marissa a riding lesson."

"You could cancel," Brant said.

He could…but he'd made a promise. "I said I'd be there."

"Having integrity can suck sometimes, hey?" Brant said, and grinned. "That sentimental heart of yours just might get smashed some more."

"Yeah," Grady said and locked the stall. "It just might."

Marissa was awake and outside when Grady's pickup pulled up the next morning. She was on the porch, sipping tea and ignoring the toast she'd prepared. He came through the gate and stood by the bottom step. He looked gorgeous, in worn jeans and a black shirt. But she stayed strong.

"What are you doing here? Again, I might add."

"I like to consider myself a man of my word," he said evenly. "And I promised you a riding lesson this morning."

"I'm not in the mood," she replied. "For you, or a lesson."

"Ebony needs the workout," he said and rested a foot on the step. "And you said you wanted to learn. So, go and get changed."

Marissa grabbed her tea and uneaten toast and moved inside, cursing him under her breath the whole time she was pulling on jeans and a shirt and her boots. By the time she got back outside, he was by the small horse yard and shelter, had haltered the horse and had the saddle and other gear ready for her.

Marissa tacked Ebony up herself, refusing to ask for his help even when the old mare bloated out so she couldn't get the girth hitched up.

"Press your knee gently under her belly," he suggested. "She'll get the message soon enough."

Marissa did as he said and it worked. Once the horse was tacked up and the bridle was in place, she walked the mare around the yard for a couple of minutes before she swung into the saddle. Grady led her to a flat, grassy spot behind one of the greenhouses and instructed her to take the mare out in a circle.

Half an hour later she had to admit he was a good teacher. He was patient and considerate and didn't push her to do too much. And Ebony was a dream. She remembered how he'd brought the old mare over to her all those weeks ago. He'd accused her of being ungrateful and they'd parted badly that day. Insults and arguments seemed to be the general tempo of their relationship. Except for that one incredible afternoon when she'd felt more connected to him than she ever had to anyone in her life. He was a generous and skilled lover and she had experienced pleasure so acute it still made her light-headed thinking about it. But it wasn't enough. It couldn't be enough. If she let it be enough, she *would* be settling.

"You're a fast learner," he said as she dismounted. "Good job."

"Thanks. Hopefully being a fast learner will help me become a good farmer," she said as she led Ebony back to the stall.

He caught up with her quickly. "Is that really what you want, Marissa? To become a farmer and live here alone?"

"I'm not alone," she said and patted the marc's neck. "I have Ebony."

She tied the mare to the railing and quickly slipped off the saddle. Once she'd brushed her down, Marissa took off the bridle and opened the gate to her yard.

Grady was beside the fence. He sighed heavily. "You know what I mean."

She shrugged, led the mare into the yard and closed the gate. "I'm not afraid of my own company. And I'd rather be alone than be in a loveless relationship."

"I thought loving the girls might be enough for you," he said bluntly.

"And once they're all grown up, what then, Grady? We'll be two people who married for all the wrong reasons."

"I can't think that getting married to make my kids happy is anything other than the only reason we need."

Logic. Relentless, gut-wrenching logic. "You'll find someone else who will—"

"The girls don't want anyone else, Marissa," he said and moved closer. He took her hand in his and rubbed a thumb along her palm. "They want you. Only you. It could only ever be you."

Her heart rolled over and she took a deep breath. "Because I remind them of Liz."

"No," he said quickly. "Not because of Liz. Because of *you*. Because they have put their love in your hands. They trust you and they want you to be their mom. In their young minds, it's incredibly simple. All children really need is to feel loved and to feel safe. And they get both of those things from you."

"Stop doing that," she demanded and pulled her hand away. "Stop trying to use them as leverage to get me to agree to this."

"Since they're obviously the only leverage I have, I'll do what I have to."

Marissa wanted to shout and curse and tell him to go to hell. But there was such an earnest belief in what he was saying in his voice, she couldn't. She took a steadying breath and met his gaze. "I can't…not even for them."

"Then what?" he demanded, his eyes darkening. "What is it you want?" he asked and pulled her close. "Is it this?"

His mouth came down on hers with seductive force, and the kiss had possession and frustration stamped all over it. His tongue found hers quickly, and she didn't have the will or strength to resist. His hands moved around her back and curved over her hips, pulling her closer, drawing them together in a way that she could feel every hard angle of his body. Marissa clutched his shoulders and she arched against him. Kissing Grady was like quenching a long-endured thirst—and she wanted more.

"Grady…" She whispered the word against his mouth, completely compliant and wistful.

"I want to make love to you," he said, kissing her throat hotly. "I want it so much I can't think straight."

"I want that, too," she admitted.

They got inside the house in about thirty seconds and made it three steps into the hallway before he kissed her again. And again. Marissa's hands were feverish as she touched him, tugging his shirt from his jeans. They kissed and walked at the same time, straight toward the living room. Grady supported her weight as they dropped to the floor in front of the big fireplace, still kissing, still touching, oblivious to anything other than pure, unadulterated need.

She stripped off his shirt and clutched at him, holding him as close as she could. Her T-shirt disappeared quickly and he dispensed with her bra with amazing dexterity. He moaned low in his throat as he bent his head to take one of her nipples into his mouth. His breath and tongue were hot and erotic against her sensitive skin, and she arched her back. He caressed her other breast as he continued to gently lick one with his tongue. It was torture. Glorious, enjoyable torture that made her mindless with need. Then his mouth trailed down, lower, across her rib cage and to her belly. He circled his tongue around her navel, and the feeling was so intense she almost screamed. He unbuttoned her jeans and pulled them down past her hips and calves and then over her feet. Her briefs followed quickly and then he was kissing her lower, and lower still. Until his mouth was on her in a way that was mind-blowingly erotic and she became a quivering wreck, so gratified that she could only say his name over and over as wave after wave of pleasure rushed through her.

His mouth moved down her thighs and then up over her hips and back to her breasts, and her aching nipples begged for more. He continued like that for over half an hour, and taking, she discovered, gave its own reward. There was no mistaking the desire Grady had for her. No way to deny the way his body reacted to her pleasure. It was like a narcotic, tempting her again and again. And it gave her the courage to touch him in return, to seek out ways to drive him crazy. To tease and torment and then finally take him inside her in a way that was so intimate, so intense, that once they were spent they collapsed in a heap on the rug and didn't say a word for over five minutes.

"Are you okay?"

Grady's voice stirred Marissa from her sexual haze. "Fine. You?"

"I'm not sure my legs are gonna work for the next half hour or so."

She smiled. "We do seem to do this really well."

"We certainly do." He reached across and grabbed her hand and held it against his chest. "Does this give me any leverage?"

Marissa sighed contentedly and traced her fingertips through the soft hair on his chest. "You could probably get me to agree to pretty much anything right now."

"Anything?"

She dug her nails in a little. "Anything except that."

"You don't know what I was going to say."

"Sure I do," she replied and closed her eyes. "You were going to tell me what a great mom I would make and then say how you would be a faithful, loyal husband. Right?"

"Maybe."

"I do know that, Grady. I know you're nothing like Simon. I know you would never cheat or lie or physically hurt me."

"Then make things right," he said quietly. "Just because it's what the girls want and we have this incredible chemistry, that doesn't mean either of us is settling, Marissa. Many people start out with less when they get married."

Temptation swept across her skin. It would have been the easiest thing in the word to say yes. Refusing him was harder. But she stayed strong. He was so wrapped up in trying to make his daughters happy, he couldn't see it was a disaster waiting to happen. *Make things right.* It was as meaningless as his first marriage proposal.

"No."

He jackknifed into a sitting position. "No?"

Marissa sat up and grabbed her clothes. "You should go."

"Kicking me out isn't going to change anything, Marissa."

"It'll mean you're not here," she said and got to her feet, holding her clothes in front of herself guiltily. "And that's a good start."

Grady grabbed his jeans as he stood and then quickly pulled them on. "You're being unreasonable. I thought you..." His words trailed and he sighed heavily. "I thought you loved the girls."

"I do love them."

"But not enough to make them happy."

Marissa scowled at him. "That's a really low blow, Grady. Do you know how this sounds? Like you'd do anything for your daughters, and that includes saddling yourself with me. When we both know that if Liz were alive, this whole idea would be—"

"Liz isn't alive," he said quickly, harshly. "What do you want me to say, Marissa? That if Liz were still here none of this would have happened? Of course it wouldn't have happened. I loved my wife and I was faithful to her and our marriage. And while she was alive I didn't look at you or any other woman in that way. But she's gone," he reminded her, his voice filled with frustration and a kind of weary rage. "Gone...and I have to move on and find a different life. We both do."

Second best. A consolation prize. A mother for his grieving daughters.

And not one word about wanting *her* as she longed to be wanted.

Marissa's heart turned to stone.

"Just go."

He remained where he was, his shirt and boots in his hand, the top button of his jeans undone and his hair looking as if she'd been running her fingers through it. She began to dress and was just about to repeat her request for him to leave when there was a knock on the front door. She froze and stared at him, still half-dressed. She wasn't expecting any visitors. Marissa quickly got back into her clothes and straightened her mussed hair.

"I'll get it," he said finally and disappeared from the room.

She heard the door open. Heard male voices. And then Grady was back in the room.

With her father right behind him.

Chapter Twelve

Busted. Grady felt about eighteen years old. He knew what Rex must be thinking, and the older man had every right to have that thought. Grady remained by the doorway, thrusting his arms into his shirt and shoving his feet into his boots while Rex walked past him and into the room.

"I'd like to talk with my daughter," Rex said, unsmiling. "Alone."

Marissa was still by the fireplace. Her expression was cool and uncompromising. And looking as if she wasn't about to be swayed by anything…or anyone. "Oh, I think we *all* need to hear this."

Rex nodded slowly, came around the sofa and dropped into the seat. "Okay."

Grady stayed by the door and met Marissa's gaze. She crossed her arms and remained standing. "I'm listening."

"I was twenty-three when I met your mother," Rex explained quietly. "Janie Ellis was… She was the most beautiful girl I'd ever met. But I ain't gonna lie to you and say it was more than it was. I was in town for a couple of weeks and we spent that time together. Then I left."

"What a lovely story," she said coldly.

"I ain't sugarcoating it," Rex replied. "I was young and more interested in horses and drinkin' than settling down. I moved around a lot, working on ranches in Iowa and Missouri. And then six years back I came through town again because I was heading to Wyoming to see an old friend. I asked around about Janie and that's when I found out about you."

She didn't look convinced. "How can you be sure I *am* your daughter?"

Rex half smiled. "I got a job at the Parker ranch a couple of weeks after I got to town," he said and glanced toward Grady. "It was kinda like providence, I guess. When I found out that you and Miss Liz were friends and that Miss Violet lived next door, I knew I was doin' the right thing by staying." He sighed heavily. "And then I saw you one time you came to visit. I took one look at you and I knew. You're the spittin' image of your grandma."

Marissa's eyes widened. "I have a grandmother?"

Rex nodded. "Yep, my mother lives in Nevada. And you have three aunts and a whole load of cousins, too."

Grady saw Marissa's expression shift for a moment. Family…that's what she'd be thinking. It was what she'd always craved.

Then be a family with me…

Grady stopped himself from racing forward and taking her in his arms. She didn't want him—that was plain enough. And she had used every excuse to not accept his marriage proposal. But he knew the only thing standing in the way of them being a family was Marissa.

"Your grandma sure would like to meet you," Rex said quietly.

"Really?" Her brows rose. "And what do you want, Rex? Absolution? Forgiveness?"

There was hurt and pain and bitterness in her voice and Grady ached for her. But she had to walk through this moment on her own. She had to meet Rex halfway, or not at all.

"I only want to get to know you," Rex replied quietly. "That's all."

"To what end?" she asked. "So we can play happy-family and pretend the last thirty years haven't happened? Well, I can't do that. I can't pretend... I can't act like it's okay that you've been living in this town for six years and didn't tell me who you were."

"I couldn't," he replied. "Your aunt said you—"

"Are you blaming Aunt Violet?" she asked, eyes blazing. "It was Aunt Violet who looked after me when my mother died. It was Aunt Violet who was *here*. And she didn't just happen upon me by chance. She took me in when I was twelve years old and cared for me when I needed someone. And let's be honest," she went on, relentless. "If you *had* known about me, would it have made any difference?"

She was clearly anguished and Grady had to fight the urge he had to shield her from the pain she was feeling. But she was strong...stronger than she realized. And only if she faltered would he step in.

"I'd like to think I would have done the right thing," Rex replied.

She laughed humorlessly. But Grady wasn't fooled. She was breaking. "Well, we'll never know."

Grady's gut lurched out of sympathy for the older man and out of the need to protect the woman he loved. "Marissa, maybe—"

"You don't get to have a say in this, Grady," she snapped and then looked at her father. "In fact, I think you should both leave."

Grady expelled a frustrated breath. Rex stood up, nodded his head wearily and walked from the room. When he heard the front door open and close again, Grady took a few steps toward her and shoved his shirt into his jeans.

She was glaring at him.

"Why are you still here?"

He came to a halt. "Why are you pushing everyone away?"

"I'm not."

Grady nodded. "Oh, yeah, you are. What are you so afraid of, Marissa?"

"Nothing," she shot back. "And I want you to go."

"I'm not going to walk away from you," he said steadily. "However much you keep telling me to go. I get that you're feeling hurt and confused about finding out you have a father—a father who wants to be part of your life—but Rex isn't going anywhere, either. He's a good man, Marissa, and he deserves a chance here. Give him that chance... meet him in the middle. Stop being so stubborn and hard-headed."

Her jaw tightened. "I haven't asked for your advice."

Grady sighed heavily. "You know, not all men are out to hurt and betray you," he said, and her eyes instantly flashed to attention. "I think that somehow, while your aunt and your mom were trying to protect you, they also made you feel like no man could be trusted."

"That's not—"

"And marrying that suit probably confirmed what you believed," he said, cutting off her protest. "But we're not all tarred with the same brush, Marissa. We don't all leave. We don't all cheat. We don't all hit. Most of us try to do the right thing. But if you don't give any man a chance, how are you going to know that?" He sighed and felt his throat thicken with emotion. "Everything you want, the family you've craved since you were a little girl—it's here, right in front of you. All you've got to do is take it."

She shook her head and her eyes were shining with tears. "I can't. None of it's real."

"It's as real as you make it, Marissa. Don't turn your back on your dad... He needs you."

And I need you, too...

"Please, Grady—just go. Close the door on your way out."

Defeated, Grady sighed again, turned and let himself out. He closed the door as she asked and met Rex by the front gate.

"Is she hurtin'?" Rex asked quietly.

Grady nodded. "Yeah, but she's stubborn, too," he said and half smiled. "Kinda like her old man, I guess."

Rex grinned wearily. "Well, I can't expect her to change years of thinkin' in a week. I reckon I've just gotta wait for her to come to me when she's ready."

"I hope you don't have to wait too long," Grady said as he moved through the gate and walked toward his truck.

"What about you?" Rex asked, stepping in beside him. "You givin' up on her?"

Grady shrugged and pulled the keys from his pocket. "She's made it clear how she feels."

"I ain't askin' about her," Rex said, his eyes crinkling. "I'm askin' about you. Looks to me like you're in love with my daughter."

"It doesn't matter how it looks," Grady said and opened the driver's door. "She doesn't want what I offered."

"I'm not so sure. I mean, she's mad at you, that's obvious. But maybe it ain't what you offered," Rex said and tilted his head. "Maybe it's more in the way you offered it."

"What does that mean?"

Rex chuckled. "I've been around awhile and I still don't

know a whole lot about women, but looks to me like what you don't know...well, I reckon that would almost fill a library."

He sauntered off toward his old pickup and left Grady by his truck before he had a chance to respond. Grady waited until Rex had driven off, then got into his truck. He gripped the steering wheel and glanced toward the house. She was impossible. Unreachable. Maddening. The best thing he could do was forget all about the foolish idea of having a future with Marissa. She'd kicked him out and told him repeatedly that she wasn't interested.

Only an idiot would keep going back for more.

Grady drove to his mother's to stay for lunch and pick up the girls. His mother and Brant were both in the kitchen when he arrived and his daughters were in the playroom keeping themselves occupied.

"Everything okay?" Colleen asked.

"Fine," he replied and sat down. Then he asked a question that had been burning in his gut since he'd left Marissa's. "Do I strike you as someone who doesn't know anything about women?"

Brant laughed out loud and his mother regarded him with genuine concern.

"Well," Colleen said as she prepared a plate of sandwiches, "I imagine you know about as much as most men do. What brought this about?"

He shrugged. "Something Rex said."

"I take it Marissa still hasn't come around?" Brant asked.

"No," he replied. "And doesn't seem likely to. I thought she'd jump at the chance to be around the girls full-time. I guess I was wrong."

His mother stopped cutting the bread and the knife clanged on the counter. Grady looked across the room and saw Colleen shaking her head.

"What?" he asked.

"Rex is right," his mother said. "You don't know anything about women."

"I don't know what you—"

"If you put it like that, no wonder she turned you down. Just because Liz was pragmatic and unromantic and didn't like fuss and you agreed to get married over a beer at the Loose Moose doesn't mean all women are so easily persuaded. Did you happen to tell Marissa that you're in love with her and *that's* the reason why you want to marry her?"

Grady's skin heated. "Well…no…not exactly."

Brant laughed again. "What happened to you being the sentimental one?"

Pragmatic and unromantic? True, Liz had been sensible and thrifty. Even on their wedding day she'd complained about the cost of the bouquets and catering. He'd laughed at the time, and again over the ensuing years when she'd insisted that she didn't want or need flowers or jewelry or anything she regarded as *overcommercialized trappings.* They'd been together since high school and the tempo of their courtship had been a steady, easy kind of ride. They'd talked and planned and mapped out their life together. They'd been friends and lovers and then husband and wife, all with very little effort on his part, he realized.

You're about as romantic as a load of laundry…

Marissa's words came back and hit him squarely in the chest.

I'm a girl… I believe in all that stuff. And I want it. I want the flowers and the music and the poetic love notes and all of that sugary nonsense…

He'd dismissed it at the time, going back to using logic and her love for his daughters as a reason for them to get married. And every time she'd refused him. Even when it was obvious they were perfect for one another. Okay…

maybe *perfect* was a stretch. Maybe it was more like want and need and desire and a kind of soul-wrenching longing that had somehow turned into love. At least, for him. And Grady had been so wrapped up in wanting her and getting her to see that they could make a family together he'd been blind to one undisputable fact…she wanted more. From him. And since his pride had been battered by her refusal, he hadn't taken the time to really think about what she was saying, over and over. She didn't want to *settle*. He'd believed she'd meant *on him*. On them.

Now a surge of clarity washed over Grady and he thought about everything they'd been through in the past few weeks—Marissa spending time with his daughters, making coffee in his kitchen and admitting the truth about her ex-husband, holding his hand while his baby girl lay in hospital, her kisses… Marissa coming into his hotel room and making love with him as if they were the only two people in the world. There was truth in her touch, and what he'd felt from Marissa that day was real and earnest and from the heart. He just hadn't dared let himself see it.

And he knew why. There had been a shadow over them… Liz's shadow. Some lingering sense of regret and then, finally, acceptance, too…the realization that his wife truly was gone from his life forever. Pragmatic or not, he'd loved Liz deeply and would always carry her close to his heart. But now he was in love with Marissa.

Grady glanced up and looked at his brother and then his mother. "Do you think… Do you think she…" His words trailed off.

"Do I think she's in love with you, too?" his mother finished for him and then nodded. "Oh, yes, I absolutely think that she is."

Grady grinned. Feeling stupid. Feeling elated.

And knowing exactly what he needed to do.

* * *

Marissa finished packing up Aunt Violet's things by the middle of the week. Anything her aunt didn't want she'd been told to deliver to the Goodwill store in town. The living room was piled with boxes, and every time she walked across the rug by the fireplace she refused to think about how she and Grady had spent Saturday morning rolling around on the carpet, lost in each other.

On Thursday afternoon she went to see Aunt Violet, who was only a day away from going into her new home at the retirement complex. They talked about mundane things for half an hour until her aunt patted her arm and asked her what was wrong.

Everything...

That's what she wanted to say, but didn't.

Grady's words had haunted her for days. But she'd been so angry, so hurt that Grady hadn't told her the truth about Rex, compounded by his insistence they get married because his daughters loved her, that she couldn't see beyond anything other than the ache in her heart.

Marissa looked at her aunt and sighed heavily. "Grady thinks I'm a man-hater."

Her aunt regarded her solemnly. "And are you?"

"I never thought so," she replied. "But perhaps I spent so long resenting the fact I didn't have a father that I went looking for fault in every man I met...and then I married Simon and proved I was right."

"And maybe your mother and I didn't make it any easier for you," Aunt Violet acknowledged and sighed. "Neither of us had ever had much luck in that department."

Marissa smiled. She knew her aunt had had her own disastrous love affair many years ago. And as for her mom... Janie spent so many years harboring resentment for being stuck in a small town with a child at such a young age, Marissa knew she'd never opened her heart to let anyone in.

"So, I guess he's right about me."

Aunt Violet's expression softened. "But you don't hate Grady?"

She shook her head. "No. I've never hated him."

"Was he why you went away to college and stayed in New York?"

She shrugged. "I liked him in high school, but it wasn't serious. Just a teenage infatuation. And by the time he was married to Liz, I'd forgotten all about it. Except…Liz died, and then I came back to town permanently and things between Grady and I changed and we had nothing… *I* had nothing to hide behind. No way of stopping myself from…"

"From falling in love with him?" Violet asked quietly.

Marissa nodded. "And I don't know what to do about it. He proposed," she admitted and saw her aunt's eyes widen. "For the girls' sake. And you know how much I love them and want to be a part of their lives. But the thought of marrying a man who wants me only as a mother for his kids and as someone to warm his bed…well, I just can't do it."

"Are you sure that's all he wants?"

Marissa nodded. "Liz was the love of his life, Aunt Violet. And Grady and I…we've always had this tense kind of relationship, but it was generally civil and despite our differences we made it work because of Liz and the girls. Now that's changed forever and we can't go back to how it was." She sighed, her insides aching. "A part of me wants to say yes to him…part of me wants to take him on any terms, because the thought of not being with him, of not being with the girls, just about breaks my heart in two. But the other part of me knows that I'd be settling for a one-sided relationship. And I can't do that, not even for three little girls whom

I love dearly. Liz wouldn't want that for her daughters, and I don't want it for them, either."

"So, what are you going to do?" Aunt Violet asked.

"I'm going to try to fall out of love with him."

As she said the words she knew there was no chance of that happening.

"I don't think you should try too hard," Violet said and smiled gently.

Marissa stared at her aunt. "So...you approve?"

"Of Grady?" The older woman nodded. "How could I disapprove? He's a fine, hardworking man who clearly adores his children. And if he makes you happy..."

"But he doesn't," she said, defiant and hurting all over. "He makes me miserable."

Violet chuckled softly. "He makes you miserable because you're in love with him and want to be with him...right?"

Marissa nodded. "What if he breaks my heart?"

Violet patted her hand gently. "But, Marissa, what if he mends it?"

She left her aunt a few minutes later, with plenty to think about. Marissa hopped back into her car and headed to the gas station on Reynolds Street to fill up and buy milk and bread. Once she'd pumped the gas, she headed inside to pay the cashier and stopped in the doorway. Rex Travers was by the counter, chatting to the cashier. As though he sensed her presence, he turned and walked toward her.

"Afternoon," he said and smiled so warmly it was impossible for her to not smile back. "How are you holdin' up?"

This is my father.

It was a hard reality to swallow. As a child she'd imagined having a father countless times. But it had been a shadowy, faceless image. Not a man with kind brown eyes and an expression so sincere she felt her rage and feelings of betrayal almost seep away. She didn't want to like him.

She didn't want to think of Rex as anything other than a foreman on the Parker ranch. But he *was* more. He was her father. Her dad. *Her family.*

"I'm okay."

He nodded. "I've been wantin' to come and see you again. Would that be okay?"

Make or break. Grady had told her he was a good man. She could say no and never see him again. Or she could put aside all her anger and meet him in the middle.

"Sure," she said quietly.

For a moment he looked as though she had given him the moon, and her insides tightened.

"We could talk," he said. "That would be good."

Marissa nodded. "Yes, I'd like that."

"Me, too," he said and smiled.

She nodded again and walked toward the cashier. When she turned around after she'd paid, he was gone, and through the window she saw his truck pull away. As she drove toward home she realized she'd forgotten the milk and bread. She figured she'd go out the following day and headed east. When she got a hundred yards from the small farm, she noticed something attached to the gate. She slowed down and saw a bunch of inflated balloons flapping in the breeze and a large piece of pink cardboard that had writing on it.

M. Please go to the high school. G.

The high school? It didn't make sense. It was obviously from Grady. The two initials made that very clear. But what was he up to? She grabbed her cell and called him, but it went to voice mail. She could ignore it. But…she was curious. Curious enough to turn the car around and drive back into town and five minutes later pull up outside the high school. There were several kids milling outside the front, and a few standing around the bronze statue of a long-dead president whom the school was named after. She got out of the Volvo and walked up the path. And then she saw more balloons and another bright pink piece of cardboard stuck to a bench seat beside the statue.

M. This is where we first met, remember? Please go to the stables at the rodeo grounds. G.

Her heart almost exploded in her chest. She looked around and saw that some of the kids were pointing at her, but she didn't care. The sign was the most romantic thing she had ever seen. Suddenly excited, she raced back to her car and headed to the fairgrounds. Ten minutes later she was by the stables, staring at another sign.

M. This is where we shared our first kiss, remember? Please go to JoJo's. G.

Her knees were trembling so much she could barely make it back to her car. But another ten minutes and she'd pulled up outside the pizza parlor. The place was busy with lunch-time patrons, but she wasn't looking at who was inside… she was looking at the bright pink piece of cardboard and the large bunch of balloons attached to the shingle outside the restaurant.

M. This is where we had our first date, remember? Now please come home. G.

By the time she was back in her car, she had tears streaming down her face. She drove directly to the ranch, wiping her eyes every few minutes. She pulled up at the gates and brought the car to a stop. She took a breath, and another. In the distance she could see Grady's pickup outside the ranch house.

Make or break.

Earlier, she'd had that thought in relation to her father. But now…now it was about a future with the man she loved. A future she sensed she could take if she only had the courage to put aside her fears. She shifted gears and pressed the gas and drove down the long gravel road toward the house.

Marissa pulled up in the driveway and got out. The doors on the pickup were open and music was blaring from the radio, an old country love song about second chances. It warmed her heart and when she saw that the back of the vehicle was filled with flowers, her throat closed over. She stayed by the truck and touched a few of the blooms, figuring he must have raided every florist, gas station and convenience store in the county to produce such an amazingly romantic gesture.

She grabbed a daisy stem and walked toward the house. Other than the music coming from the radio, everything was so quiet, as though the place was deserted. Even the dogs hadn't made an appearance. Maybe she was to be sent somewhere else? She walked around the cab of the truck and ducked inside to turn the volume down. Once she was back out of the truck, she walked toward the house and listened for any noise…something to tell her that she wasn't alone at the ranch. In the distance she heard the sporadic bellow from a cow, but that was all.

She was about to climb the steps but heard something make a raspy sound beneath her feet. Marissa looked down and saw that the stairs were scattered with bright pieces of colored paper. She bent down and picked one up. It was folded in half, and she opened it. It was a note written in a dark, masculine scrawl. *You're so beautiful.* She picked up another one. *I'd like to watch you sleep for the rest of my life.* And then another. *I'd even eat overcooked steak for you.* Her eyes filled with tears as she wrinkled the notes in her hand.

She climbed the steps and came to a halt outside the door. There was a sign stuck to it, bigger than the others, only this one had crayon pictures drawn on it, too. Colorful murals clearly done by young hands. But it was the words that captured her heart.

M. This is where I fell in love with you. Marry me. G.

She was crying now and didn't care. The words were all she needed.

"Marissa?"

She heard his voice, felt his presence as if it was air she needed for her lungs. She glanced to her left and saw him coming around from the side of the house. He looked so good. So strong, and yet in that moment, adorably vulnerable. He'd stopped walking and had his hands half-outstretched.

She sucked in some air and managed a tiny smile. "So, I guess you kind of love me?"

His chest expanded as he drew in a short breath. "Yeah."

Marissa shuddered emotionally. "Well…that's convenient."

"It is?" He took a step closer. "Why?"

"Because," she said and smiled, her bottom lip quivering, "I kind of love you, too."

And then she was in his arms. He was holding her. Kissing her. Crushing her against his chest as though he couldn't get her close enough.

"Tell me I'm not dreaming," he whispered raggedly against her mouth.

"You're not dreaming," she assured him and held on to his shoulders. "You really went to all this trouble for me? The signs, the music, the flowers…everything?"

He grinned ruefully. "You said I was unromantic. I had to prove to you that I can be whatever you want."

"I adore what you did…really, it's the most romantic thing anyone has ever done for me. But don't change too much," she said.

"I promise I won't," he said and kissed her again, making her breathless.

Marissa's knees wobbled. "Grady, shouldn't we—"

"You want to talk?" he asked, cutting her off so gently that her heart surged with love for him. "You want to get all the serious stuff out of the way before we go inside and tell my daughters, my mother, my brother and your father that you have agreed to marry me?"

Marissa's gaze narrowed. "They're all inside?"

He nodded. "Lying low until I say the word."

She grinned. "You are so bossy and arrogant sometimes."

Grady laughed. "Sometimes. And you did just agree to marry me, right?"

"I think so," she replied and smiled. "I know so."

"Good," he said and led her to the wicker love seat by the door and started to draw something out of his pocket. "Because I have something for you that I—"

"Talk first," Marissa said and tapped his hand lightly before he had a chance to remove anything from his pocket.

He nodded again and sat beside her. "Okay...talk."

Marissa gripped his hands, so happy she thought she might burst. "Are you really sure about this, Grady?" she asked. "About us?"

"Never surer," he replied. "I know what I want. And who. I love you, Marissa...right here, right now and for all the days of my life."

"And Liz?" she said, saying words she knew needed to be said.

"I'll always carry her in my heart," he acknowledged softly. "She was my wife and the mother of my children. And she wouldn't want either of us to spend our lives alone."

"But she—"

"I knew her," he said gently, gripping her hands. "*We* knew her. We knew her kindness and her generous spirit. So maybe, a lifetime ago, she kept some things to herself that made all our lives turn out a certain way...but I can't regret that. And neither should you. I loved her. I grieved her," he said, swallowing hard. "But now I love you."

She sighed and met the love in his eyes. "People will talk. You know that, right?"

He shrugged. "People generally do. And if you mean the O'Sullivans, as long as they stay clear of you and at least pretend to respect our relationship, I'll have no beef with them. But they're still my daughters' grandparents and Liz's family, so I'll do what I can to make sure the girls spend time with them."

"I agree," she said, loving his compassion for a family still mourning the loss of a daughter and sister they had adored. "Liz would want that, despite the differences she had with her parents over the years."

Grady's eyes darkened. "Speaking of parents…how are things going with yours?"

She smiled. "I guess Rex told you we talked today?"

"He mentioned something. Are you feeling okay with it all?"

Marissa shrugged a little. "Yes, much better. What you said to me the other day made me think long and hard about things…about my past…about how I put my trust in the wrong man and in some part of me it did validate every belief I'd had about trust and betrayal."

Grady raised her hand to his mouth and kissed her knuckles. "I'll never hurt you, Marissa, and I will always protect you from anyone who tries."

Heat pricked behind her eyes and she took a short breath. "You've taught me to trust, Grady. I fell in love with your goodness, your strength and your integrity. And every time I see you with the girls I fall in love with you just a little bit more."

His eyes glittered brilliantly. "One day soon," he said,

his voice filled with promise, "you and I are going to add to this little family of ours."

Marissa smiled. "You really want more children?"

"Absolutely," he said and grinned. "Three boys, to make it an even half dozen. And now I'm going to do what I should have done a week ago," he said and dipped back into his pocket, pulling out a tiny velvet box as he dropped to his knee beside her.

"And what's that?" she teased, touching his handsome face lovingly.

"I'm going to ask you to be my wife, the right way this time. I love how you make my daughters light up when you walk into the room. I love how you have the most generous spirit of anyone I have ever known. I love how you're stubborn and make me crazy sometimes. But mostly, I love you because of the way you fill my heart, Marissa. Marry me?" He opened the box and Marissa saw a beautiful pink solitaire diamond. "The girls picked it… Milly said it matched your sparkly cowboy boots."

"I love it," she said, her eyes shining brightly with tears as he slipped the ring on her finger and moved to sit beside her. "And I love the girls. And I love you, Grady, and I can't wait to be your wife. So, yes, I'll marry you."

He kissed her then, long and sweet and full of promise for the future.

"We'd better get inside and tell them," he said and grinned. "Before my mom's face is pressed against the window behind us."

Marissa laughed. "I really like your mom."

"Well, she really likes you, too," he said and got to his feet. He pulled her up gently. "In fact, I reckon you've just about got every Parker wrapped around your beautiful fingers."

She laughed again. "Oh, you've done your share of that, too. Anyhow, it goes both ways."

"It certainly does. Let's go," he said and opened the front door, and all Marissa heard as they walked through the door were delightful squeals of laughter. All three girls came racing down the hall, their arms outstretched. Breanna and Milly hugged her tightly as Grady hauled Tina into his arms.

"Daddy," Milly said, all smiles. "Does this mean Marissa is going to be our mommy?"

Grady grabbed Marissa's hand and linked their fingers. "It sure does."

The girls cheered again just as Colleen, Brant and Rex came down the hall to greet and congratulate them. This was her family. And in that moment, she felt and shared their joy and happiness. And their love.

Epilogue

Marissa couldn't wipe the silly smile off her face. It was her wedding day. And truly the happiest day of her life.

They were getting married seven weeks after Grady had proposed. Well, proposed *properly*. She still melted inside when she remembered how utterly romantic his proposal had been. He didn't like being reminded about his earlier attempts to win her over. But Marissa liked teasing him just a little…especially when they were curled up in bed together. At her place, of course. He had very strict ideas about what was proper when it came to sharing a bed around his daughters. Not until they were married, he'd said.

She'd found a buyer for her aunt's ranch quicker than she'd expected. A lawman from Detroit who'd taken a job with the police department had purchased the place unseen and would be arriving the following week. And since Grady's ranch felt more like home than anywhere ever had, she was looking forward to moving in and starting her new life as his wife and as a mother to the girls. He'd already discussed plans about building her a studio behind the house, and Marissa had found his enthusiasm infectious. She wanted to get back into her craft as soon as she could, and Grady had been incredibly supportive.

So, here she was, on the first Saturday in winter, wearing the most gorgeous long-sleeved ivory lace gown that Colleen had helped her choose from a boutique in Rapid City, and that she'd cheekily decided to team with her pink cowboy boots.

As expected, the kids were over the moon and were excited about being flower girls. Brooke had agreed to be her bridesmaid and Brant and Tanner McCord were the best man and groomsman, respectively.

The wedding ceremony and reception was taking place at the ranch beneath a huge white tent. About one hundred people would be attending, mostly family and friends of the Parkers. But Marissa didn't mind. The Parkers were now *her* family, and she loved them all dearly. Especially Grady and the three little girls who had every part of her heart. They hadn't invited any of Rex's family to the wedding, as it was too soon for Marissa, and Rex had understood. But she and Grady, along with Rex, were planning a trip to Nevada the following month to meet them, and she was very much looking forward to it.

"You look amazing."

Brooke was in the doorway, dressed in a pale lavender satin halter-style gown that had a matching wrap.

Marissa smiled. "Thanks. It still feels a little surreal."

Brooke checked the thin watch on her wrist. "Well, in about twenty minutes it will be real enough," she reminded her and walked into the room. "Wait until Grady sees how beautiful you look."

"Are you two ready?"

Lucy Monero, who'd arrived to help Colleen and Brooke

get the kids ready, was now standing in the doorway. Lucy Monero had become something of a frequent fixture at Colleen's place in the past few weeks. Grady had laughed about how his mother was matchmaking again—this time with Brant and the pretty doctor. Lucy didn't seem to mind. However, Brant appeared to be even more subdued than usual around Lucy.

Marissa was certain it would all work out. She was too deliriously happy to imagine that it wouldn't.

Brooke grabbed the tiara and veil from the bed. "Just about," she said and placed it securely on Marissa's head. "There...all done."

Marissa smiled. It felt good having friends again. Brooke and Lucy had welcomed her wholeheartedly into their circle, and she genuinely liked both women. "Thank you."

"Colleen just left with the girls, and she said to tell you she'd see you at the ranch," Lucy said and grinned. "Oh, and your dad's here."

My dad...

Things had developed steadily with her father over the past few weeks. It still seemed a little strange to think of Rex in terms of being her parent, but they were slowly building a father-daughter foundation.

When she asked him if he would like to give her away at the wedding, there had been tears in his eyes.

Someone cleared their throat and she saw Rex hovering by the door, dressed in a pale gray suit, white shirt and bolo tie.

His weathered but still-handsome face crinkled.

Marissa took a deep breath and turned toward her father. "Well...I guess we should get going."

She waited for his reply, saw his brown eyes shine just a little. "You look beautiful, kid."

She swallowed the lump in her throat. Rex had gotten

into the habit of calling her *kid*, and she didn't mind the endearment. It was kind of sweet. Things between them would probably never be perfect, but they were both trying to find the middle ground where they could have a real relationship with one another. Grady's love and commitment had helped her realize she could have Rex in her life and let go of the past. Even Aunt Violet seemed to have warmed toward the older man. And it was, she realized, as she let herself get drawn into another hug with her father, a whole lot more than she'd imagined she would ever have.

She blinked away the heat in her eyes. "Thank you."

Rex stepped back and gripped her shoulders. "Your momma would've been real proud of you. And the way you've taken to lovin' those little girls makes me real proud, too. He's a good man, kid…one of the best I've ever known."

"Thank you. That means a lot to me."

Once he'd released her and left the room, Marissa's mouth etched into a wide smile.

Things *really* did have a way of working out.

Grady was nervous. He pulled at the tie around his neck and swallowed hard.

"Don't worry," his brother said quietly as they stood at the altar. "I'm sure she'll show."

Grady gently elbowed Brant in the ribs. "I don't doubt it for a minute."

Brant grinned and then said more seriously, "I see Kieran O'Sullivan is here."

"He's a friend of Marissa's."

"And the rest of your in-laws?"

Grady shrugged lightly. "Some things are simply too hard to face, I guess."

Brant nodded. "You know, I think Liz would be okay with this."

"I think so, too."

He believed it. Felt it deep within his bones. Liz had known how special Marissa was. That was why they'd been friends. He remembered Liz telling him how Marissa was the most elementally good person she had ever known. And he understood that now. The way she was with his daughters made it crystal clear. Marissa was kind and caring. Marissa loved deeply, and he was humbled and thankful that she had placed that love with him.

Most of the guests were seated in the marquee and music had started playing. The celebrant who would officiate the ceremony was checking his watch again, and it made Grady smile. He spotted his mother at the end of the seating rows, organizing his daughters in turn to walk down the aisle. Watching them made his heart flip over. They looked deliriously happy as they headed toward him in their fluffy dresses, tossing tiny petals from the baskets they each carried.

Brooke followed the girls down the aisle, and he winked at his cousin as she rounded up his daughters and kept them to one side.

And then he saw Marissa.

Love for her warmed his blood as she walked down the aisle beside her father. He never failed to be riveted by her beauty and the kindness in her expression. Before she moved beside him, she headed for his daughters and kissed each one on the head gently. He loved that about her...loved how she made his children feel as though they were special and loved. Then she was beside him, and he grasped her hand. "You're here," he said softly.

"Yes," she replied as the music began to fade. He said thank-you to Rex and squeezed Marissa's fingers gently. He knew how hard she'd been working to have a relationship with her father and was incredibly proud of her strength and commitment.

"You look beautiful," he said so only she could hear as they turned toward the celebrant. "Have I told you today how much I love you?"

Her brown eyes shimmered. "I'm not sure…"

Grady smiled at her teasing. "I love you, Marissa," he whispered. "So very much."

"I love you, too."

"So…are you ready for this?" he asked as the music finally stopped.

"Absolutely," she said and ushered the girls closer while they spoke their vows.

And that, he thought, was about as good and as real as it got.

* * * * *

Don't miss Brant Parker's story,
the next installment of Helen Lacey's new miniseries,
THE CEDAR RIVER COWBOYS
Coming soon to Harlequin Special Edition!

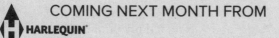
Available January 19, 2016

#2455 FORTUNE'S PERFECT VALENTINE
The Fortunes of Texas: All Fortune's Children • by Stella Bagwell
Computer programmer Vivian Blair believes the secret to a successful marriage is compatibility, while her boss, Wes Robinson, thinks passion's the only ingredient in a romance. When she develops a matchmaking app and challenges him to use it, which one will prove the other right...and find true love?

#2456 DR. FORGET-ME-NOT
Matchmaking Mamas • by Marie Ferrarella
When Dr. Mitchell Stewart begins volunteering at a shelter alongside teacher Melanie McAdams, he falls head-over-stethoscope for the blonde beauty. Once burned in love, Melanie's not looking for forever, even in the capable arms of a man like Mitchell. Can the medic's bedside manner convince Melanie to open her heart to a happy ending?

#2457 A SOLDIER'S PROMISE
Wed in the West • by Karen Templeton
Former soldier Levi Talbot returns to Whispering Pines, New Mexico, to make good on his promise to look after his best friend's family. The last thing he expects is to fall in love with his pal's widow, Valerie Lopez. Now, Levi's in for the battle of his life—one he's determined to win.

#2458 THE DOCTOR'S VALENTINE DARE
Rx for Love • by Cindy Kirk
Dr. Noah Anson's can-do attitude has always met with success, both professionally and personally. But when he runs up against the most stubborn woman in Jackson Hole, Josie Campbell, nothing goes the way he planned. It will take a whole lotta lovin' to win Josie's heart...and that's what he's determined to do!

#2459 WAKING UP WED
Sugar Falls, Idaho • by Christy Jeffries
When old friends Kylie Chatterson and Drew Gregson wake up in Las Vegas with matching wedding bands, all they want to say is "I don't!" But when they're forced to live together and care for Drew's twin nephews, they realize married life might be the happy ending they'd both always dreamed of.

#2460 A VALENTINE FOR THE VETERINARIAN
Paradise Animal Clinic • by Katie Meyer
Single mom and veterinarian Cassie Marshall swore off men for good when her ex walked out on her. But Alex Santiago, new to Paradise and its police department, and his adorable K9 partner melt Cassie's heart. This Valentine's Day, can the doc and the deputy create a forever family?

REQUEST YOUR FREE BOOKS!
2 FREE NOVELS PLUS 2 FREE GIFTS!

⬥HARLEQUIN®

SPECIAL EDITION

Life, Love & Family

YES! Please send me 2 FREE Harlequin® Special Edition novels and my 2 FREE gifts (gifts are worth about $10). After receiving them, if I don't wish to receive any more books, I can return the shipping statement marked "cancel." If I don't cancel, I will receive 6 brand-new novels every month and be billed just $4.74 per book in the U.S. or $5.49 per book in Canada. That's a savings of at least 12% off the cover price! It's quite a bargain! Shipping and handling is just 50¢ per book in the U.S. and 75¢ per book in Canada.* I understand that accepting the 2 free books and gifts places me under no obligation to buy anything. I can always return a shipment and cancel at any time. Even if I never buy another book, the two free books and gifts are mine to keep forever.

235/335 HDN GH3Z

Name	(PLEASE PRINT)

Address	Apt. #

City	State/Prov.	Zip/Postal Code

Signature (if under 18, a parent or guardian must sign)

Mail to the **Reader Service:**
IN U.S.A.: P.O. Box 1867, Buffalo, NY 14240-1867
IN CANADA: P.O. Box 609, Fort Erie, Ontario L2A 5X3

Want to try two free books from another line?
Call 1-800-873-8635 or visit www.ReaderService.com.

* Terms and prices subject to change without notice. Prices do not include applicable taxes. Sales tax applicable in N.Y. Canadian residents will be charged applicable taxes. Offer not valid in Quebec. This offer is limited to one order per household. Not valid for current subscribers to Harlequin Special Edition books. All orders subject to credit approval. Credit or debit balances in a customer's account(s) may be offset by any other outstanding balance owed by or to the customer. Please allow 4 to 6 weeks for delivery. Offer available while quantities last.

Your Privacy—The Reader Service is committed to protecting your privacy. Our Privacy Policy is available online at www.ReaderService.com or upon request from the Reader Service.

We make a portion of our mailing list available to reputable third parties that offer products we believe may interest you. If you prefer that we not exchange your name with third parties, or if you wish to clarify or modify your communication preferences, please visit us at www.ReaderService.com/consumerschoice or write to us at Reader Service Preference Service, P.O. Box 9062, Buffalo, NY 14240-9062. Include your complete name and address.

HSE15

Turn your love of reading into rewards you'll love with

Harlequin My Rewards